T0340927

THE BOOK OF RAMALLAH

The Book of Ramallah

EDITED BY MAYA ABU AL-HAYAT

Part of Comma's 'Reading the City' series

First published in Great Britain by Comma Press, 2021.

www.commapress.co.uk

A CIP catalogue record of this book is available from the British Library.

ISBN: 1912697424
ISBN-13: 9781912697427

This book has been selected to receive financial assistance from English PEN's 'PEN Translates' programme.

The publisher gratefully acknowledges the support of Arts Council England.

Contents

CONTENTS

Introduction

SOME CITIES ARE BUILT from scratch, on empty land. Some seem to have always been there, deriving their importance from their unique location. While others exist only in the imagination, the stuff of legends and tales handed down by grandmothers. Ramallah is not like any of these; a seemingly modest city with a short and relatively peaceful history, it is a city of ordinary stories, rather than heroic myths. To its many, regular visitors, it's a relaxing place to spend a summer vacation; to its residents, it's just home. Historians define it as, originally, merely a village near Jiffna, outshone by all the other Palestinian towns, with their richer histories and captivating legends, cities such as Al-Quds,[1] Nablus, Jericho, Al-Khalil,[2] and Gaza. Nonetheless it has remained stoical and quiet in its resistance as well as a welcoming place to live.

And yet, with its unassuming nature and convenient geography – sprawling along a ridge of the Samarian Hills, nearly 3,000 feet above sea level – Ramallah has managed to take its place as a pivotal city in modern Palestinian life. To historians from afar, this might seem like an accident, but it's an accident that a lot of thought and planning has gone into.

Located in the heart of the West Bank, 16 kilometres north of Al-Quds, Ramallah's city limits cover an area of approximately 18,600 dunams[3] and provide home to 70,000 people. Around it are an additional 80 satellite villages, refugee camps and other small hamlets. The Governorate of Ramallah and Al-Bireh (it's neighbouring city) is home to 370,000 residents in total. Indeed the boundary between the cities of Ramallah and Al-Bireh is indistinguishable; the buildings and streets of the two cities intertwine making them feel like one city. And even though Al-Bireh is larger, both in area and population, 'Ramallah' is the common name for the wider conurbation. In reality, the two cities are two completely different places, under two different local administrations with different economies, cultural traditions and social attitudes. Let's put it this way, you can sip a glass of whiskey in a bar in Ramallah, something that you could never do only a few metres away in Al-Bireh.

Ramallah is host to several important government ministries, not least the Mukata'a compound[4] the Palestinian Legislative Council Building[5] and the headquarters of the Palestinian Security Services in the West Bank. This means that Ramallah is the political centre of modern Palestine – a kind of de facto, if unrecognised, capital. The only thing that casts this status in doubt is the historical and political status of Al-Quds among Palestinians. Perhaps because of this uncertainty, Palestinians, in general, have an ambivalent relationship with this city, which acquired its pivotal status only after the Oslo Accords, in the so-called 'Oslo Years' (1993-2000). This ambivalence to Ramallah and its status is part and parcel of Palestinians' ambivalence to the Oslo Accords themselves, which created a short-term peace (of sorts), and allowed for some self-government, but led to no long-term plan, or any restoration of the kind of free movement enjoyed by Palestinians before the First Intifada. (Although Ramallah was designated an 'Area A', in the Oslo II Accord, meaning it had full civil and security control, and was out of bounds for Israelis, the Israel Defence Forces (IDF) still dominate the network of roads surrounding it, many of which are bypasses that only Israeli citizens can use, servicing the many expropriated land settlements that have sprung up throughout the West Bank in the years since Oslo).

To many writers, Ramallah is an ideal, a dream, a promise. Many expatriates returned to the city in the 1990s, in the wave of optimism generated by Oslo, having spent decades in exile, longing to return to at least part of their homeland. Their expectations on returning were sky-high, and were only shattered by the reality they found in the on-going occupation. In his novel *I Saw Ramallah*, the late poet Mourid Barghouti experiences this moment, looking at the gun being carried by the IDF soldier at the crossing: 'His gun took from us the land of the poem and left us with the poem of the land. In his hand he holds earth, and in our hands we hold a mirage.' Ramallah represents this mirage, this glimmer of hope that isn't real, to many writers. Indeed the popular use of Ramallah in the title of recent novels builds on this set of expectations Palestinian readers have of the city: *Ramallah Dream* by Benjamin Barthe; *Blonde Ramallah*, and *Crime in Ramallah* by Obaad Yehya and so forth.

Looking back through history, references to Ramallah can be found in records as old as Crusader artefacts. Archaeological evidence suggests there was a village here at least as early as the 16th century, under Ottoman rule, and that it began to thrive towards the end of that era, with the first town council recorded convening in 1908. The name 'Ramallah' can be traced back to at least 1186 and is formed from the conjunction of the words *raam*, meaning hill, and Allah, meaning God. Thus the importance of 'God's hill' might always have been its geography being perched on a hilltop ridge, with cool updrafts, and spectacular views in all directions. People in Ramallah will swear that, standing on their roofs they can see the beaches of Yaffa, Akka and Haifa, beauty spots most Palestinians can never see.

When you travel to Ramallah from the south, from Al-Quds or Al-Khalil, before you reach it you are confronted with a crowded road, traffic jams, a checkpoint, towering buildings and chaos everywhere. You know immediately that you have arrived at the famous Qalandiya Checkpoint, separating Ramallah from Al-Quds. If it weren't for politics, the journey between the two cities would take just 15 minutes, but in reality it takes 1½ hours. From the checkpoint you pass through Al-Qalandia Refugee Camp and then Kufr Aqab which eventually brings you to Al-Quds Street which is officially the entrance to Al-Bireh. For all intents and purposes, though, you can say you are now in Ramallah.

Alternatively if you travel to the city from the north, after similar, if less famous, checkpoints, you pass through the villages of Birzeit and Jifna until finally you reach Al-Irsal Street, to be greeted by the infamous Mukata'a complex where Arafat was besieged by the IDF for two years and almost entombed by the Israeli bulldozers. Then you head for the heart of the city, to a confluence of roads and noise that people call Al-Manara Square, where today four lions sit or stand in various poses. Originally the monument consisted of five lions at the base of its pillar[6] which, according to legend, represented Jerias, Shqair, Ibrahim, Hassan and Haddad, the five families descended from Rashid Al-Hadaddin, who is said to be the progenitor of all the Christian families that founded the city. The story goes that 'Rashid Al-Hadaddin fled from Al-Karak (in present-day Jordan) in the middle of the 16th century after a disagreement with a Muslim family there. He led his small caravan across the barren hills of Jordan to a forested area 16 kilometres north of Al-Quds and, between the caves and remnants of Roman villages, the caravan settled and built their new home.'

The oral tradition indicates that Rashed Al-Hadaddin later returned to Al-Karak, but his five sons were determined to stay in Ramallah and so became the grandfathers of its people and the namesakes of its lions.

Al-Manara roundabout is at the meeting point of six roads, the foremost amongst them being Rukkab Street, named after the famous ice cream parlour, known for selling the tastiest ice cream in Palestine.

As Al-Manara is the destination of many roads, so Ramallah seems to be the destination of many people new to the country. Travellers come first to Ramallah and rest here, before exploring further. As one folk song puts it: 'Where to? Ramallah! Tell me traveller, where to? Ramallah! Do you not fear Allah, tell me traveller, where to? Ramallah!'[7]

Among such travellers was Palestine's most famous literary son, the poet Mahmoud Darwish. Returning from his exile, he settled in the Al-Teerah district and worked in the Khalil Sakakkini Cultural Centre in the Masyoun district. On Ramallah's streets, you might also catch a glimpse of other writers who have returned, like the poet and novelist Zakaria Mohammed who, after 25 years of exile in Tunisia, returned. You might see him walking on Maktaba Street, for example, or heading down to Ramallah Al-Tahta[8] where you can find street vendors selling falafel, hummus and grilled meat. There you might also bump into the short story writer Ziad Khadash sitting with a group of writers in the Insheraah Coffee Shop or the Ramallah Coffee Shop. If you're lucky you'll see the serene figure of lawyer and author Raja Shehadeh, passing through the streets with such gentle politeness you would hardly even know he was there. Or perhaps you will catch sight of architect and author Suad Amiry on her way to the Riwaaq Centre for Architectural Conservation, or Salim Tamari on his way to the Institute for Palestine Studies. There are authors on every street, this being a city teeming with culture where not just writers and artists have made their home, but also arts organisations. Here you will find the Abdel Mohsen Qattan Foundation, the Al-Qasabah, the Al-Sareyah, the Cooperation Institute, the Palestine Writing Workshop, the Tamer Institute for Community Education and nearby in Birzeit is the Palestinian Museum and Birzeit University.

This is Ramallah for you: a horizontal city – ranged along the contours of a hilltop ridge, where so much is new – surrounded by much more vertical cities, whose topography tips over the sides of steep, vertiginous valleys, or gathers around mountain tops, cities deep with history.

It is a city of contrasts, with a sophisticated café culture and modern restaurants as well as working-class falafel shops and markets. A city of businessmen and NGO staffers, modern companies and haphazard buildings that almost obliterate the historic limestone houses hidden among them, with their ancient, subtle architecture whose original families have since been lost to the diaspora. It is a city with three refugee camps in its centre: Al-Am'ari, Al-Jalazon and Qalandia. A city of deprivation and neglect, not to mention continuous raids, demolitions and arrests by the IDF.

People commute from the towns and villages to the north and south for work, many of them living in Ramallah during the week and only returning to their homes at the weekend. So come Thursday night[9] the place changes, almost becomes a ghost town compared to the hustle and bustle of mid-week. Ramallah is also home to many foreign NGO employees who add a different vibe and way of life and also add a premium to the price of everything. So the city has a new class of middle-income workers struggling to pay off loans for luxury cars and other consumer products.

Ramallah is also a city of aspiring pop groups, hip-hop producers and experimental musicians who you might see perform at venues such as The Garage or Radio or Al-Muhatta or Shams. It's a city of performance artists, theatre producers, film-makers and actors, many of whom can be found in cafés like Zamaan and Al-Inshiraah.

Because of all of this, it is also the city that is always testing how far it can go, experimenting with what's possible, and being judged in the process. A place of tension as well as excitement, with its many tower blocks and mosques, churches and bars, and where gunfire can always be heard in the distance, resounding to a backdrop of curfews, arrests, sieges, strikes and martyrs.

The stories gathered for this anthology highlight the contradictions that make up Ramallah – a modern city but an occupied city; a home but also somewhere to escape. Roads feature prominently in many stories, including the time of the Second Intifada (2000-2005) when the official routes between Ramallah and the neighbouring towns were blocked or too dangerous, necessitating unusual modes of transport for hundreds of commuters – like donkeys to traverse the dirt tracks and circuitous mountain routes – who would arrive at their workplaces in ministries and corporate offices splattered with mud. This was a profoundly traumatic time for all Palestinians, which saw the invasion of Ramallah and a two-year-long siege of Palestinian Authority President and PLO leader, Yasser Arafat in his Mukata'a compound and curfews that could last for over two months. This era is the setting of Ibrahim Nasrallah and Khaled Hourani's stories – a time when love and death competed for the heart of the city. In Ibrahim Nasrallah's historically accurate, but seemingly implausible 'Love in Ramallah', we read about love stories blossoming in very different places: on the road from Nablus to Ramallah and in the city itself; always outside, never indoors. We read of the man who is forced by Israeli soldiers to kiss a girl he doesn't know so their packed bus can pass through a checkpoint, and of the man who blows a kiss to his wife through the window as military jeeps invade their neighbourhood to make an arrest. In Hourani's story, 'Surda, Surda!... Ramallah, Ramallah!', a man tries to finish his physiotherapy session in the Mukhmas building on Al-Irsal Street before Ramallah closes down for yet another curfew, but ends up being stranded at the clinic with other patients unable to leave.

Ahlam Bsharat's story is set much closer to the present day, in the current pandemic, and the only one in the book set wholly indoors. It depicts the isolation of a woman who has left her village to work in Ramallah, now living alone in a flat in Umm Al-Sharayet, one of Ramallah's more run-down neighbourhoods. Denied the love and companionship of an ordinary relationship, she embarks on an affair with a horse. In the surrealism of Bsharat's well-woven tale we could be forgiven for thinking this love story is the city's only reality.

Ameer Hamad takes us back to the roads, in particular the chaos of the route between Ramallah and Al-Quds, where Ramallah might seem like a city in a bubble floating on air, compared to the harsh reality of Qalandia Checkpoint. Where you wonder what fate has in store for you, every time, as if it's the first time.

In Anas Abu Rahma's tale, the protagonist is a villager who yearns to see the sea, in a city very far from it, and to be loved by a city girl before strange nightmares overcome him. Ziad Khadash's story, 'Get Out of my House', tells of a man who comes home to find a strange woman in his house who is adamant that it's her house and that he has to leave before her husband returns. Here we glimpse the ephemeral life of the refugee, returning from his home in the camp, leaving his library behind to be ruined by soldiers going through his stuff, and living alone in a city he doesn't belong where he has to continually prove his identity or his innocence. The issue of identity resurfaces in Mahmoud Shukeir's story where the protagonist tries to convince himself that he is a man of the city now and that he can do anything that the city's residents do. Set in the 1960s, before the occupation of the West Bank, when Ramallah was under Jordanian rule but with Israel's expansionist war drums beating over the horizon, it portrays secret political parties and movements and the first acts of resistance heralded by revolutionary communiqués and protests: a time when identity transcended all other tensions, such as that between town and country.

Liana Badr's story 'A Garden that Drinks Only from the Sky' goes to the roots of life in Ramallah and the unique experience of being occupied. Here we see the Ramallah that has its land expropriated for the construction of Israeli settlements that now surround it on all sides. In this story, we meet Najaah living in her house on the western reaches of the city, making all her food at home from the bounty of the small plot of land that she lives off, along with her mother: Labnah, cheese, apricots, olives and home-baked bread. When the rain stops falling on her tiny paradise, she travels to the Ibrahimi Mosque in Al-Khalil to pray to Allah for the rain to return and there she finds love for the first time.

The tales of independence, personal identity and individuality in this collection mirror the allowances Ramallah makes for your life. It is a city that allows you to think freely, unlike many other Palestinian cities. But it also questions absolute freedom from the outset by asking about the limitations on freedom and what is acceptable, what is original and what is incidental, what is real and what is as Barghouti says, a mirage. It brings us to the bigger and much more intractable question (as Palestinians we are obsessed with the big questions): what kind of a Palestine do we want as a people and as individuals – as artists, writers, blacksmiths, carpenters, politicians, business owners, prisoners, the lost and the found? A Palestine in our image, far from the vision others want for us to embody? Ramallah is a city that is being suffocated by settlements and checkpoints from all sides, yet is filled with a desire to open up and advance. It is a city with an ability to adapt and blend in, to take on the forms around it, and it has enough hustle and bustle to let you disappear in it and feel like you have all the freedom in the world. And yet it can deprive you of this freedom as quickly as you turn a corner.

Maya Abu Al-Hayat, October 2020
Translated by Mohammed Ghalaieny

Notes

1. Jerusalem.
2. Hebron.
3. A unit of area with Ottoman origin. In Palestine, a dunam is equal to 1000 square meters, or 0.1 hectares.
4. Muqaata'a is a generic name for the central administrative building in Palestine. Al-Muqaata'a in Ramallah was the Palestinian Authority HQ and also where the offices of President Yassir Arafat were.
5. The Legislative Council is the Palestinian parliament.
6. For a full history of the lions of Al-Manara Square, see https://www.palestine-studies.org/sites/default/files/jq-articles/26_shibli_1_0.pdf
7. Wein a Ramallah, 'Where to, Ramallah?', a song made popular by the Jordanian singer Salwa Al-Aas.
8. Lower Ramallah.
9. The start of the Muslim weekend.

Love in Ramallah

Ibrahim Nasrallah

Translated by Mohammed Ghalaieny

1

WARDA KNOCKED AT UMM Walid's door and the woman emerged moments later.[1]

'*Ahlan wa sahlan.*[2] What can I do for you, my child?'

'I heard there is a young man, a bachelor in your house,'[3] said Warda.

'Well, he's not exactly young,' Umm Walid said with bemusement, adding, 'What do you want from him?'

'Just so there's no confusion, could I check, is he called… Yasseen?'

'Yes he is,' Umm Walid nodded.

'Well that means he's young!' Warda exclaimed.

'But you really should meet him before proposing to marry him, don't you think?!'

'No, it really isn't necessary! Is he here?'

Umm Walid shook her head.

'If he is actually here but is just hiding then tell him that a girl will picket your house until he agrees to marry her!'

'Is that your final word then?' asked Umm Walid.

'Final!'

'If you were enquiring about anyone other than Yasseen I would have said you were crazy.'

Warda smiled: '*Al-hamdulillah*, that puts my heart at ease.'

★

When Umm Walid related the tale to Yasseen he couldn't stop laughing.

'It's a good sign don't you think?' she asked.

'I wonder how she found our house.'

'She said she learnt of you from the play about your life and your years in prison, and that she felt the genuine article would be even better. So she followed her heart here.'

After a long silence he asked, 'But, what did you think of her?'

'Honestly?'

'Of course!'

An even longer silence elapsed and then a smile spread and filled her face, and she said, 'To tell you the truth, I liked her.'

So he said, 'I wanted to say the same thing, even before I've met her!'

2

'By Allah, your age is showing, Na'eem,' Yasseen said.

'We've all aged,' replied Na'eem. 'You don't even play football with me anymore! Do you remember how you used to take me and the other local kids out to play every week? And now you're back to take their children out.' Then he added: 'What about your kids? Isn't it time for you to get married and have some?'

'Me? Nah, our people don't need one more widow and another set of orphans. There is enough suffering here! You're the one that should get married.'

'No, I've missed it, my friend, and I'm not talking about the train.' Then he laughed. 'Don't take me seriously.'

'If you had said anything else, I would've said prison had changed you,' Na'eem replied.

★

The bus to Ramallah had to stop at an Israeli checkpoint between two hills, a place called Uyoun al-Haramiya.[4] There had never been a day when soldiers hadn't been stationed at this spot. First it was the British soldiers; after them the Jordanian soldiers and now here we have the Israeli soldiers. Yasseen knew all this.

'One day we will have a checkpoint here,' Na'eem said.

'Can you see how grand our ambitions are now?' Yasseen retorted.

They ordered the passengers off the bus. Then a soldier boarded it and walked the length of the aisle until he reached the long back seat. Then, from inside he looked back out at the faces of the passengers lined up on the tarmac looking for any expression other than indifference.

The soldier got off the bus and circled around the passengers, stopping beside an attractive young girl to stare at her. He walked a few steps then stopped again. Turning, he signalled to three other soldiers, observing the scene from 15 metres away, to come closer.

As they approached he walked to the end of the line of passengers and stopped by Yasseen and Na'eem, signalling to Na'eem to step forward.

Na'eem knew all about checkpoints. He knew every one, from his earliest days they had been in his face, waiting for him. From experience, he knew that at this time of day the soldiers like to toy with the passengers for their own entertainment, to treat them as their playthings.

The heat at 4.30 in the afternoon was enough to ignite the air between the two hills. Yasseen took a look at the line of cars piling up behind the bus. A person needed no superpowers to hear the silent curses emanating from their eyes, the body language that betrayed a frustration with everything around them.

'COME!' the soldier barked at Na'eem who hadn't moved.

The soldier stopped directly in front of the attractive young girl, and there behind him now stood Na'eem. The soldier turned, looked at Na'eem, then looked back to the young girl. 'Do you want the bus to pass?' he asked Na'eem. Na'eem nodded in affirmation.

'If you want the bus to pass, you have to kiss her!' the soldier said, pointing at the girl.

A glimmer lit up the soldiers' eyes. They liked this game, it enthused them. The passengers by contrast looked at one another bemused. As for the young girl, the whole thing was like a shock to her.

A car horn behind the bus broke the silence for a moment.

'Who's that khmaar[5] beeping?' yelled the game master, heading back towards the car. The driver tried in vain to convince him that the horn had gone off by accident, but the soldier insisted that the car leave the long queue, turn around and go back to where it came, Nablus.

'If you want to sleep the night here, then stay, or you can go back to Nablus. But there is no Ramallah for you today, understood!?'

A few minutes later the car and its passengers were heading away from the checkpoint, back to the other checkpoint they had just left behind, the three kids looking out of the back window trying to figure out what had just happened.

The game master turned back to Na'eem and said, 'Do you think it's over? It is up to you. You Palestinians are always talking about making independent decisions. Well, if you want the bus to pass and for the cars behind it to pass, then do as I say.'

The young girl poked her head above the surface. Until this point she'd been submerged in a lake of shame. With eyes pregnant with tears, she looked at Na'eem who looked as if he were in an even bigger lake of his own.

Admittedly, for all his knowledge of checkpoints, he'd never contemplated a scenario like this. He looked to his friend, Yasseen, finding him lost as if in a daze. Just before Na'eem turned back to face the soldier, Yasseen locked eyes with him for a moment. Then the soldier pressed him: 'Have you decided?'

'I won't do what you ask.'

'I told you, you're free khabibi,[6] don't kiss if you don't wanna kiss. But if you and the others do want to pass through here, then kiss her.' Then, as he walked away, he added: 'Don't move from where you are. Stay put.'

In front of the checkpoint, the soldiers were giggling to themselves. Rummaging for change in their pockets and passing it around, they began placing bets on whether he would kiss her or not. He will kiss her, the game master said as he pulled some cash from his pocket and flung it on the sandbags. The sun was beginning to set and the passengers felt like they were suspended in time. The soldier approached Na'eem again and asked, 'Haven't you decided yet?'

'I won't do as you ask.'

And so the rifle butt struck his thigh. Everyone heard the thud on his femur before he fell to the ground, only for the soldier's jackboot to follow up, landing in his stomach.

'We're busy here, I told you if you kiss her you all pass. If not you sleep here.'

'I won't do as you ask.'

The soldiers protested this foul play by the game master;

his use of violence could change the outcome of the bet. But he was deaf to their complaints.

Another blow came. Na'eem tried to dodge it but there was no escape; blood spurted from his forehead. The soldier walked away. Things felt like they were about to explode. The lined-up passengers were getting restless as they watched the scene without being able to move. Passengers from several of the cars and buses had disembarked on either side of the road. Now the guns turned to them; the soldiers ordered them back to their cars.

In a turn that nobody saw coming the young girl bent down by the man on the ground in front of her, took his hand and whispered, 'Kiss me, I beg you!'

Na'eem looked up at the passengers again; they were staring at the ground trying to not be there.

He kissed her on her right cheek. As his lips met her face several of the soldiers whooped, as if they were cheering for a winning goal scored by their team, while others grumbled in disapproval.

★

As the bus rolled past the checkpoint, the passengers' eyes reflected a mixture of shame, oppression, anger and disapproval. They stared brokenly at the floor; silence was the new passenger they had taken on.

The young girl raised her head, while all the other heads were lowered. She looked at the young man who, as if he could feel her gaze, raised his own head and looked back at her. And so it was till the last stop.

The passengers left their seats, followed by Yasseen. The only two people left on the bus were a young man and a young girl.

3

Umm Walid always knew when her nephew had arrived when she found a bouquet of roses on the windowsill.

At first, she would admonish him: 'Why the roses? They must have cost you a fortune!' But then she started getting used to them. She would miss them whenever Yasseen was late bringing in a new bouquet for her. The roses would dry out but she would keep them and keep waiting, and waiting.

'You know, I now wait for the roses like the trees await the rain. My heart sings when I see them!'

'I promise you, the vase will never be empty of roses.'

'But doesn't it bother you to bring them all the way from Ramallah?'

'No, but the glances I get from the passengers do. It confuses me, Umm Walid, that someone can carry a sack of molokhia[7] or onions from Jenin to Rafah[8] without anyone raising an eyebrow, but when I bring a bouquet of roses, everyone starts eyeing me up as if I am in my birthday suit.'

'Does it embarrass you?'

'No, it never embarrasses me, but it irks me that roses are so alien. The moment we leave Ramallah, silence takes over, and it's almost as if I can hear their theories and questions: "The roses are for his wife," one thinks, while another: "No one gives his wife roses these days. He must be going to a wedding, or a birthday" And a third "Could it be this old fox has forgotten he's no longer a teenager and fallen in love?!"'

'Oh Yasseen, may Allah have mercy on you. People are kind-hearted and don't think like that!'

'People – not just here, but in many places – find it easier to curse than be kind. Have you ever seen a plane dropping roses on a city?'

'Of course not.'

'But you've seen a plane dropping bombs?'

'Often.'

'You see! The world is crazy. How about you! How many times have you told Abu Walid that you love him, in public?'

'Goodness! In front of people? I've never even told him I love him in private!'

'Ha! But if you had, why wouldn't you say it in public?'

'Do you want them to say I am crazy?'

'You see! This is what I'm trying to say. Our shame of beautiful things surpasses our shame of the truly shameful. Either way, I will keep on bringing you roses, tormenting those who find it strange that I am carrying them all the way from Ramallah.'

'Do you mean there are people who don't find it strange?'

'Sometimes. Once, after staring at me and the roses for a while, a woman sighed then said to me: "I envy her, she's lucky." I asked her, "Who do you mean 'she'?" So, she said, "The one you're taking the roses for." So, I told her, "No, I am the lucky one, to have her." To which she said: "Then she's doubly lucky, to have you and to have your roses."'

Then Umm Walid looked at him: 'Why don't you settle down, Yasseen?'

'Believe me, if I settled down I would go crazy.'

*

Under the midday sun glinting through clouds, in front of the two almond trees that shaded the lower yard of her house now destroyed, beneath a flock of house sparrows hovering above the damaged power lines watching cautiously for the yard to be clear of kids, Umm Walid gazed into the distance. She looked past the clutch of children playing in the dirt yard; there were less of them today than usual. Looking up at the towering sky, she saw three kites soaring. Then she turned her eyes to her neighbour's window, the pane punched out by a missile that went on to rip through the kids behind it, all were waiting for their mother to make them breakfast before going to school.

Umm Walid went back to looking into the distance. She could see the children playing. Today they seemed to be playing with the kind of joy they felt the very first time they played. She didn't know what number they needed to make two teams to chase a ball around, so she carried on staring into the distance...

The children's cries brought her back to earth. She swept her gaze swiftly among them until she settled at the far edge of the yard where Abu Walid sat, along with a group of men who were consumed in a conversation so familiar to her that she could probably guess every word.

150, maybe 200 metres was all that separated them, no more.

A noise she knew well took swung her attention to the end of the road. An army patrol, four jeeps roaring up the road towards her, choking the alley with their black smoke. Here they are again, occupying everything.

Yasseen's face swung into her line of sight, then disappeared.

The clamour of the jeeps brought her back to their street. They were now next to her house, parked close to its northern side.

But the children didn't stop playing. They carried on as if the place had never seen a soldier. There, above the wires the caution that had set into the wings of the sparrows was noticeable.

Umm Walid returned her gaze to the far side of the yard. The men had stopped chatting as they sensed something was happening on the other side of the wall, they knew nothing of it but were slightly reassured that the children were still playing.

She saw Abu Walid waving at her from afar and waved back. The soldiers noticed their gestures. Yasseen's face passed by again, but this time it didn't disappear. She saw him heading down the stairs towards the lower yard and for a moment, she envisioned the yard as it always had been, green and well kept.

She could hear her voice flowing through her body like a river, rising from the depths of her heart, filling her lungs as she called, 'Abu Walid!'

From the other side of the yard, came his voice, as if he'd been waiting for her call for a long time: 'What is it?'

'I love you, Abu Walid. I love you!'

The soldiers watched this old woman calling to her man before their eyes switched to the other side to see him say, 'What?'

'I love you,' she said again.

Abu Walid shook his head. He squinted a little but his eyes shone with an unusual glimmer as he read the faces of his companions.

He lifted his head and, for a moment, it seemed as if the children had stopped playing, and the sparrows didn't know which way to fly.

As for the soldiers, they were holding their breath.

Abu Walid realised that the whole world had stopped and was waiting for him. He looked to the far side of the yard, where the woman, proud and tall like a pine, was waiting and he called:

'I love you, Umm Walid!'

'What?' she responded, even though she'd heard it loud and clear the first time.

'I love you!'

And everything settled down.

He observed the silence that his voice had created in the space. 'She got the message, loud and clear,' he whispered to himself with a quiet joy, as he returned to his seat. At the same time, the patrol leader shook his head in confusion: 'An old man, an old woman, shouting "I love you" at each other. Crazy fucking Palestinians.'

As if the pine tree within her suddenly grew higher and higher, she found herself feeling taller than any other day and, casting a compassionate eye to the other side of the yard, watched as the patrol disappeared.

Notes

1. The prefixes 'Umm' and 'Abu', mean 'Mother of' and 'Father of', respectively, usually followed by the name of their eldest son.

2. Welcome, but in a very emphatic way, short for 'you are among us as family members and your stay with us is never a burden'.

3. This is a reference of the social custom where the mothers of unmarried men are known to go enquiring to the families of single young women; only here it is reversed.

4. An Israeli military checkpoint in *Wadi al-Haramiya,* the valley of the thieves. *Uyoun* translates as wells or springs.

5. The Arabic word for donkey is *hmaar,* but Israelis mispronounce the letter *h* as *kh*, as in 'loch'.

6. *Habibi*, with added *kh* sound similar to previous footnote, literally means my love but in this context it is similar to the British English usage of 'mate'.

7. A leafy plant of the nutritious *Corchorus olitorius* species, known in English as jute mallow and found commonly across the Levant, Egypt and part of Cyprus, used in making a dark green, soup-like dish.

8. Jenin is the northernmost city of the West Bank, and Rafah is in the far south of the Gaza Strip, so saying 'from Jenin to Rafah' is like saying from Land's End to John O'Groats, with the added irony that this journey is not even possible because of Israeli restrictions on movement.

A Tragic Ending

Mahmoud Shukair

Translated by Thoraya El-Rayyes

HE LIVED IN THE city now. But he still felt like a villager, like a simpleton or a bumpkin. Walking down the street, he thought about the neighbour's daughter who had suddenly appeared by his front door as he'd been leaving, as if she'd been tracking his movements in and out of the house. She said her parents were out and wouldn't be home before evening, that she would like to invite him over for coffee in the garden. Hatem said he was going to watch the game and wouldn't miss it for anything, ignoring the reproachful look that entered her eyes, then left. As he neared the Manara roundabout, he thought about the secrets this city hid from him in its crevices. The neighbour's daughter was trying to impose herself on him, just like Aziza. But Aziza had been different, he'd never forget her, no matter how far away he got. He thought about her for a while, and that village, then snapped back the people and sights around him.

Hatem stopped in front of the bookshop window and inspected the book titles. He didn't see anything new. *[He did this, occasionally, to give the impression that he was an intellectual to the customers of the café next door seated on the pavement. Just as a sense of self-loathing would start to wash over him, he would walk away.]* Someone started to call out to him, it was Muawiyah walking over:

13

'You must be off to the match!'

'Yes, you?'

'I haven't decided yet. When does it start?'

'At four.'

'So we still have an hour. Let's go for a walk until then.'

Hatem knew what Muawiyah was up to. Since he had announced he was planning to run for office to replace that MP who had died, he'd started roaming the city streets with workers, tradesmen and petty bureaucrats. He thought it was a way to attract voters, to give the impression that he was a humble man of the people. *[Muawiyah, yes! I know exactly who the narrator is talking about. Even after all these years! Still a big admirer of himself, always trying to be noticed. Sometimes playing the role convincingly but mostly making a hash of it.]* They passed the Manara roundabout: Hatem looking around absently, Muawiyah loudly pontificating about 'the nation' and 'the people' so everyone could hear, Hatem then trying not be embarrassed by this contrived attempt to play on people's emotions. As the clichés continued to spout from Muawiyah's mouth, Hatem made a point not to say a single word. When it was almost time for the match to start, Muawiyah said, 'I just remembered something important, I have to go visit Qaddoura Camp.'

'Alright.'

Hatem felt like a nightmare had been lifted from his shoulders and headed to the football pitch desperate for some light relief.

Free Entertainment

The balconies facing the pitch were packed with women. He slowed down as he glanced at them, a clash of emotions erupting in his chest. He wished Aziza were standing on one of those balconies *[Her house doesn't have a balcony, only windows]* so he could wave at her, so that she could come

14

down after the game and they could walk together under the trees whose branches reach all the way down to the pavement. So that they could go back to his room and she could undress in front of him however she liked and he could observe her body. They would spend some time together, walk back out into the street, the neighbours would still be sitting on their balconies under the autumn sky. He would feel a little shy, he is shy, especially when it comes to women. At the start of their relationship, he had been extremely shy and only became less reserved when Aziza started pursuing him. Their love affair had been going on for a while when he told her, 'We're going to get caught up in some scandal.' She wasn't concerned, didn't care about the consequences this would have in their remote, little village. He told her, 'I like your nerve, I'm going to write a story about you and make the ending a tragedy.' She asked why, and he said, 'Literature needs these kinds of endings.'

He walked past the balconies, past the women's eyes fixed on the pitch. The boredom of their lives was so intense that these matches had become one of the few places they unearth some joy. Hundreds of teenagers climbed to the top of the wall around the pitch and street vendors set themselves up at the best spots to sell nuts and sandwiches. He scanned the crowds who had come from the city's different neighbourhoods and nearby refugee camps to watch the game. The enormous mechanic caught his eye, the match jester. Hatem watched him rip his shirt off and jiggle his belly as he cheered for the team from Jelazone. *[The mechanic lived in the city, but his loyalties were with the camp].*

The game started and the ball flew toward a defender from Jelazone who kicked it hard and watched it fly into the sky, leave the pitch entirely, and bounce on the corrugated iron roof of the nearby parking lot. *[The narrator wants to illustrate the innocence of the game Hatem had watched that day in the 1960s. In his mind's eye, he compares this to the ones he watches on TV nowadays featuring stars like Paolo Rossi, Maradona, Zidane and Ronaldo].* The mechanic jiggled his belly at the Jelazone defender:

'Careful brother, you're not playing with the parking lot!'

A wave of laughter rose up, the laughter of people hungry for even the simplest amusement. Tens of children ran after the ball to throw it back onto the pitch. The game continued, lackluster, until Jelazone scored their first goal. Ramallah's coach burst out into the middle of the pitch, enraged, as people in the audience yelled:

'Offside! Offside!'

The coach and the referee locked horns in a heated argument and chaos flooded through the crowd, as people started rushing onto the pitch. A vicious brawl broke out and police cars arrived, men descending from them armed with shields and truncheons. The balcony women hid inside their houses, following the events from the corners of their windows.

Hatem left the ground like the defeated hero of a story, walking forlornly down the street, upset at what had happened. The shops, the trees and the balconies all seemed like they were dressed in black. He approached a curve in the road that led into the narrow street ending in his house. When he saw Adli Khader loitering in the street, a sharp shiver travelled down his spine. God, he hated that man. He curdled the blood. Ever since Hatem moved into the city, Adli would follow him whenever he saw him.

He quickened his pace and turned into the narrow street before Adli could get any nearer *[I know exactly who this informant is, even though the narrator has changed his name.]* After he had gotten some way down the street, he looked over his shoulder and saw Adli standing at the curve in the road, his eyes brazenly following Hatem.

An Ambiguous Relationship

He stood, alone, behind the window. The darkness of the night was faded by the street lamps, and by the light shining from windows and balconies. He looked over at the next building and saw her saunter from her bedroom to the balcony in her nightgown. He figured she could see him but was pretending she couldn't. *[This was one of the cruelties of the city, or rather the cruelties of its women which, maybe, makes them more seductive.]*

He had watched her since he moved in, admired her from the first moment. He decided to have a silent conversation with her through the window, maybe she would respond. He would keep watch for her in the street and followed her a few times as she glided along like a fish. He yearned for her, developed an attachment to her. Aziza had once asked him, 'When are you going to get married?' He replied, 'I don't know, but I'll only marry a city girl.' *[Maybe he had gotten this idea from novels.]* 'Forget the city, and those city girls! Are city girls marriage material?' Aziza had said.

Like a naïve teenager, he intentionally ran his hand through his hair. The girl was looking out from the balcony, scanning the neighbouring buildings without focusing on anything in particular. When she saw him raise his hand, she stepped back and turned away, switching off the balcony lights and closing the curtains. *[It hadn't occurred to him that she hadn't admired him since that first moment too. He didn't find out until later that from that moment, she'd crossed him out of her thoughts once and for all.]*

He retreated to his room, pacing from one corner to another. He heard the neighbour's daughter from inside her house. She was intentionally raising her voice so he would come out to see her. He had never taken a liking to her, even though she was so kind-hearted that it verged on stupidity. Her legs were covered in thick hair that she didn't bother to remove like other women did, and she shaved the hair on her cheeks with her father's razor, leaving behind cuts that couldn't be covered up by makeup. He noticed all of this very keenly.

Her voice faded after a few attempts and he began to breathe more easily. Then there was a quiet knocking at the door: Bahjat and his wife, it seemed they had come to visit him together to throw informants off, pretending they were on a family visit. They walked into the room and sat on the two discoloured wooden chairs, as he sat on the edge of the bed. Bahjat was silent for a few moments.

'Welcome!'

The wife was silent, as if she didn't approve of this visit, or maybe she didn't want to get on her husband's nerves by interfering in his business. Bahjat said, 'You look tired. Are you in pain?'

'No, I'm upset by what happened at the game.'

'With everything we're living through, that kind of thing is expected. As you know, our oppression sets us up to be defeated.'

He guessed why Bahjat had come to visit him, and Bahjat didn't wait long. He took some underground publications out of his pocket, told Hatem that he'd been approved for party membership and when the first meeting would be held. Hatem was thrilled as well as slightly terrified.

On his way to the meeting, Muawiyah – standing in a shop doorway – spotted him:

'Come, come in, I'll introduce you to the owner. He used to be in the party with us.' *[Muawiyah had also been a party member, but resigned out of fear of being arrested.]*

'Please, I don't have time.'

'It seems you're going on a date.'

'You want to mess around, and I'm in a rush.'

'Listen, I know what happened at the match. I'm going to tell you something I'd prefer not to tell the voters: the reason for all this tension is the absence of women.'

'You're worried they'll kick up a fuss that you'll never hear the end of?'

He let out a soft laugh, and Hatem walked off to his first party meeting at Arizona Café.

Meeting on a Rainy Day

The Ramallah rain hammered down, washing the streets, trees and orange-tiled roofs of the city. Young women took shelter on their balconies, savouring the feeling of standing behind the glass as they watched people run through the downpour. The eyes of the neighbour's daughter followed Hatem as he left home. The cafés closed their glass doors, enclosing their customers in a warmth fused with sad memories.

Adli Khader found himself having to shelter from the rain by stepping into the waiting room of the bus company. Sitting on a bench, he watched the monotonous routine of the street through the wet glass and even fell asleep, for a few moments, to the sound of the car tyres driving through puddles and splashing the pavements. Hatem hurried past and Adli Khader snapped to attention, stood up, opened the glass door, and contemplated following him before being discouraged by the heavy rain. He sat back down on the bench and dreamt of a bygone era when he was just a child running through the rain.

Hatem turned toward Cinema Al-Jamil. Mu'tasem, the comrade he'd met at Arizona Café a few days ago, waited for him by the cinema entrance. Mu'tasem saw him approaching from a distance and started to walk in front of him, on the left side of the small street in the shadow of its buildings. Hatem walked further behind, following him carefully. There were only a few people out, maybe because of the rain. Hatem started to feel nervous and walked even closer to Mu'tasem as they entered a dark passageway leading to a first floor flat in one of the buildings. Hatem, concealing his unease, commented:

'It's a secure flat.'

Mu'tasem laughed and introduced him to three comrades with stern, alert faces *[as if they were about to change the world]*. Everyone welcomed the new comrade and the meeting began.

Beginning of a Tragedy

As was to be expected, life had acquired a different kind of flavour. The only thing left of his old life was Aziza – an unrealised dream that now he tried to forget by standing at his bedroom window for hours on end looking at a woman living opposite. *[At the end of the day, Aziza was just a simple village woman who never thought to spray perfume on her neck or under her bra.]* He observed the slim young woman who, as usual, moved backwards and forwards between her bedroom and the balcony. She had continued to ignore him, gave him no attention at all. One evening, he'd heard singing coming from her house. All the rooms were brightly lit and the neighbourhood's women had shown up in long, embroidered dresses with bright sash belts. The teenage girls by contrast arrived in modern clothes revealing their cleavage and legs.

An overwhelming curiosity came over him and he left his room, hoping not to run into the neighbour's daughter. Last night, he'd caught her lifting her dress to reveal her legs and fleshy thighs. It didn't escape his attention that there was a femininity about them, something carnal. But then he remembered the razor and immediately lost interest. She had quickly lowered her dress, as if surprised that he was walking toward her and he'd hastily disappeared into his room. Tonight, luck was on his side; she wasn't at the building entrance. He walked along the street, passing the girl's house where children were playing and asked one of them, 'What's happening here?'

'A wedding, Randa's wedding.'

'Who is she getting married to?'

'Her cousin, he came from America and he's taking her with him.'

Randa! Her name is Randa and she's leaving the city. Could it be? *[She had never become attracted to him, despite his many failed attempts to get her attention]*. He felt dejected. He knew he would always be a pathetic villager in this city, otherwise she wouldn't have rejected him. He wandered aimlessly in the streets and came across Adli Khader near the Manara roundabout but paid him no attention. In fact, he hoped the informant would follow him.

He headed to Itha'a Road looking tortured. Did things between him and Aziza have to end the way they did? At first, she had spent weeks calling out to him from her window. When he didn't respond *[out of fear and a lack of experience]*, she had started to pass by his window armed with all kinds of excuses, whispering shyly at first. With time, she spoke more boldly, said that her heart had been drawn to him since the first moment she saw him enter the village. She said she was excited for him to teach her how to read and write, so she could write her name next to his. She said she liked to lay her head on his chest, and fall asleep there a little.

He glanced back, and saw the informant following him at a distance. He had a nagging urge to spite him and headed toward a narrow, unlit street. Adli followed him like a shadow. Let him do what he likes, Hatem was feeling brave. He hadn't been brave with Aziza, always afraid of a scandal. Aziza wasn't afraid of anything, the recklessness of her attraction to him had scared him. Every now and then a kind of vague pain would take hold deep inside him, and he would decide to break things off with her. He would go back on his decision at her insistence, and things would go back to how they had been between them, neither of them knowing where they were heading.

One evening, she'd invited him to her house. She had started to take off her clothes as he watched her ample figure revealed from under the embroidered peasant dress. They heard some soft knocks at the door and flinched. They listened for a few moments. The knocks returned:

'Aziza!'

'Oh damn it, it's him. He said he'd be away for a week, and it's only been a few hours.'

Agitated, she threw her dress back on. She opened the door and didn't see anyone. A few moments later her husband walked in from the back door and saw an open window. He looked out but didn't see anyone in the darkness. He looked for a rope in the corner of the room, fiercely ripped her dress off, tied the rope around her arms and legs and dragged her to bed. He lit the kerosene lamp, tore the scythe down from the wall and held it over the flame. He started to touch her stomach, and the tops of her thighs as if touching her body for the first time in his life. Minutes later, there was a terrifying scream, the neighbours opening their windows to find out what was going on.

Hatem unconsciously started to walk faster. He turned toward Batn al-Hawa, crossed the street and took a left toward the headquarters of the bus company. He approached Cinema Duna, passed Arizona Café and turned into the street leading home. *[Oh, the story. I'll give it another ending. How about something like: He contemplated her submissive body and conflicting feelings rose within him – love, pity, compassion, lust. He untied her, passionately entered her and then burst into tears].* He stopped for a moment before walking into the house, seeing Adli standing at the curve in the road, his neck tilted to the right.

A Woman's Oath

He wakes up, or maybe dreams that he has woken up.

A persistent knocking at the door. He is flooded with fear. For the last few days, the city streets had been filled with protest. The mechanic had joined in one of them – thinking it was something like a football match – took off his shirt, danced in front of the soldiers, and was pierced by three bullets in the chest. They were protests against the Jordanian government's policies. The border villages were exposed to enemy attack *[the enemy who, in just a few months, had invaded Ramallah, Al-Quds, Bethlehem, Al-Khalīl, Jericho and Gaza]*. A wave of arrests. A few days ago, he had slunk off at sunset to attend a meeting at Mu'tasem's flat that had been arranged a couple of weeks before. A rush of terror flooded his body as he approached the flat; the windows were closed, no one was there. He turned back nervously: the city streets almost empty, army tanks parked in the squares. Curfew would be starting soon.

Dull, persistent knocking. Is it the neighbour's daughter? He gets out of bed, or maybe dreams he is getting out of bed, stretches his arm toward the door but it doesn't open, hears a woman's voice, Aziza's voice. The door opens and she stands there, coming to him in the early morning with all her feminine desire. She takes a couple of steps toward him and he wraps her in his arms.

'Oh God. Show me your body so I can see how you were mutilated.'

'What are you talking about, Hatem? No one mutilated me, I swear, no one.'

'Have you forgotten that night? Isn't that what your husband did after I jumped out the window?'

'You didn't jump out the window. And my husband didn't do anything I didn't want.'

'How can I believe you? What happened to you still tortures me.'

'You're the one torturing yourself with that story you wrote. It's been bothering me since I read it. I told you to rip it up, but you wouldn't listen.'

'I told you I wouldn't rip it up, I wrote a new ending.'

'I don't care about the first ending or the second. I'll put your mind at ease now, I'll free you from your torture.'

She slips out of his arms, heads toward the bed and slowly, sensually slips off her clothes. His left arm reaches out to close the door but it doesn't close. He heads toward the bed, and there, finds the neighbour's daughter laying on it, completely naked.

Secrets Stroll the City's Streets

Ahmed Jaber

Translated by Adam Talib

'GOOD MORNING. God give you strength.'

'And to you,' the street-sweeper replied to the young woman, then silently to himself: 'God bless your every step.' On a street corner in downtown Ramallah, this scene is repeated every day at the same time, with the same characters – Abu Ibrahim and the young woman – the only things that ever change are the date and what the woman is wearing.

Abu Ibrahim was two months into his sixth year working as a street-sweeper in the district. He woke up early each morning and greeted us all, rousing the roosters and imploring the skies, before turning to me, Ramallah, to say, 'Here we go, Gorgeous.' Then he would start sweeping my streets and alleys, whisking away any trace of the night before and preparing me for the day ahead. Cloaked in my new finery, I watched as the houses stirred, their windows thrown wide like eyes, their doors yawning. It was finally my turn to wish the people a good morning.

Every day, I played the goddess, observing my people closely and exchanging secrets with them. For example, today the young woman abandoned her heart on a street corner – I won't tell you which one because that's strictly between me and her – before heading on her daily visit to the shops that squat hidden behind the brand-name outlets. When I lost track of her, all I had to do was look for the clashing bright colours she was known to wear and then I found her easily. She went from shop to shop until she'd finished her rounds and then before returning home she went back to that very corner, the one that only she and I know, and picked her heart up again. Then she ran back home. This morning, she had stopped by her usual coffee guy – in Ramallah, everyone has their favourite coffee guy – and although she knew his coffee wasn't the best the city had to offer, she and the other customers liked it enough and the prospect of changing their routine was too much of a drag. That's all there was to it. She had simply become a regular.

The coffee guy didn't have time to chat with his customers. He barely had time to ask them what they wanted and to hand them their order because the whole operation took no more than three minutes. He allowed himself to ask each of his customers just one question and that was how he heard about the day's news. His customers were a pretty diverse group: they included economists, politicians, engineers, businessmen, labourers, students, and so on. He also asked everyone how they were doing and everyone gave the same answer, 'Good, thanks.' He always hoped that one of them – man or woman – would ask the same of him but they never did. I, Ramallah, asked him all the time, however. Every evening as he wiped down his coffee cart before shutting it, he would answer me: 'I'm fine,' he'd say and then he'd smile and whisper to me. I'm not telling you what he said – it's a secret – but it always made me laugh.

After he finished his morning shift, Abu Ibrahim walked down Rukab Street, with a slight but perceptible limp, toward the coffee guy because he was a regular, too. He peered into the shop windows as he strolled past before a poster stopped him in his tracks. Well designed with eye-catching red text, the poster advertised a music festival that was happening in a few days. After he'd noted all the details, the time and the location, which like most musical and artistic festivals was in the area between Rashid al-Hadadin Square and the Ramallah Cultural Center, he recalled an event from ten years ago.

Abu Ibrahim calls his sister on the phone. 'I'm taking you to a concert tonight.'

'A concert? Are you serious?' she asks. 'Why me? Why don't you go with your wife?'

'Because this concert is for us. We're the ones who used to dance to Boney M. songs in the 70s.'

'Boney M.! When?'

'Tonight. They're here for the Palestine International Music and Dance Festival. We can relive our days of dancing to 'Daddy Cool' and 'Rasputin'. We can be kids again.'

The band comes out on stage to cheers and applause that lasted far longer than they expected. 'We love Palestine!' Maizie Williams shouts into the microphone. 'We love you all – people of Palestine! We're going to take you somewhere far away. To the sea!'

Every detail of that night will remain clear: how he loses his voice; how he dances like he hasn't danced in years, holding his sister's hand like he did thirty years before. He will never forget the moment when the power goes out and he laughs and screams, 'Welcome to Palestine!' Then the electricity kicks back in and with it all the colourful lights, the euphoria, the twirling plaited hair, and the Casio watches all the kids are wearing.

Abu Ibrahim emerged from his daydream and carried on walking. He saw grains scattered carefully on the street corner. He always wondered who it was who came to leave wheat for the pigeons. That person created an image for anyone who walked past, a painting of pigeons calmly eating their meal, unstartled by the footsteps on the pavement. He still didn't know who this person was, he realised, and at that moment he resolved — like someone deciding on a new adventure, if you could call it that — that he would wake up even earlier the next morning in the hope of meeting the pigeons' friend.

The next morning at 6am, Abu Ibrahim steps out of his house into the darkness and heads toward the corner where the pigeons' friend leaves wheat for them. He looks at the face of the sky, which is still freckled with stars. He sees an orange light peeking out from a bakery nearby so he runs over quickly to say, 'Good morning, neighbour,' and then returns to his route down Rukab Street. He looks over his shoulder at the streets he has to sweep and says to them, 'I'll be back, Alleyways. I just need to satisfy my curiosity first. I won't be late, my lovelies.' As he walks, he imagines what the person he's searching for might look like. *It'll be someone gentle with delicate features and we'll become friends*, he whispers to himself. He arrives, limping as usual, at the pigeon corner and notices that there's no wheat on the ground. He's elated. In a few minutes, he will finally meet his new friend. He decides to wait in the doorway of a nearby shop and sits down, but it isn't nearly as easy as he'd expected. The pain in his foot causes him to shut his eyes before he can settle into his new position. He takes an old radio out of his jacket pocket, presses the button, and extends the antenna. Fairouz begins to sing: *I asked you, my love, where are you going to?* A quarter of an hour passes and still no one has come. He stands up and looks into the distance, first to his right and then to his left. Perhaps he'll see the pigeon's friend coming. But he doesn't see anyone interesting-looking, which is how he imagined the person would appear. He sits back down in the doorway. A grey pigeon lands on the ground in front of him and searches for any grain leftover from the day before. When it fails to find any, it returns to its companions who are all perched on the heads and backs of the lions in Al-Manara Square. Their little eyes are fixed on their corner of the road, waiting for their friend to come and scatter wheat for them. He examines the empty streets, which remind him of the First and Second Intifadas. These streets were full of rocks and planks and the remains of burnt tyres back then. He remembers the days and nights he'd spent fighting to keep the Israeli Army Jeeps from entering the city. He thinks about everything he did for me, the city he loves. How he defended me as a resistance fighter and how a bullet in his upper thigh had caused the limp he has now, how he refused to leave me to go work in the Gulf, and how these days he wakes up earlier than most of his neighbours in order to get me ready to meet them like a son changing places with his mother.

He stands up, his eyes misty, and turns to walk back toward the area where he works. Before he's even taken two steps, he hears a voice calling him. 'Hello there!' It's a voice he knows perfectly well, but he doesn't turn around and he doesn't return the greeting. He carries on walking, confident that the pigeons will be fed and pleased to have discovered their friend's identity. Only when he arrives at his own patch does he say to himself, 'Cities have to know how to keep secrets, don't they, Ramallah?'

'Yes, my son.'

Get Out of My House

Ziad Khadash

Translated by Raph Cormack

I NEVER THOUGHT THAT, one night, I would go home to the wrong house. How funny and surreal it would be to end up in some other house on some other street and come across some one else, who I didn't know sleeping in my bed and reading my books. Even at my most drunk, I could always find my way home easily; I just let my nose take me there, guided by the smell of the big lemon tree, half of which stretches over my window sill and whose branches reach my desk. I can smell it as far away as al-Manara Square. I remember, many times, following the invisible trail of that familiar smell, making my way home, with a feeling of majesty that I could not explain.

The petrified woman now standing in front of me was holding a kitchen knife and getting ready to scream. Desperately fumbling for her mobile phone, she put one hand over her heaving breasts. She too never thought that, one night, she would go home to the wrong house. Here I was, coming back after a night out with friends. I was feeling neither happy, nor particularly sad. I was coming back from my parents' home and thinking about my books, which the Israeli soldiers had confiscated during a raid on the refugee camp. I just needed a hot bath, dinner and then sleep as soon as possible. But suddenly, there was a woman in front of me. And I was in front of her.

'Excuse me, Madam, what are you doing in my house?'

'What are you doing in my house, Sir? How did you get my key? Get out now, please. My husband is coming and he will think that I…'

'Are you mad, what are you talking about? Your "husband"? I should "get out"? Listen lady, this is my house!'

The woman was clearly malicious, making up some story to mess with my head. Was I the victim of a trick that my friends were playing on me? Were they all going to have a good laugh at me afterwards? I was sure that I was not dreaming, nor was I drunk and there was no question that this was my house. Why should I have to confirm the identity of my own house? I know everything in it and everything in it knows me. My books, all stolen from *my* friends; pictures of *my* dead friends, Hussein, Ezzat, and Khalil; my bed that used to be a sofa; the peeling paint of my walls; seven black hairs from the head of a girl from Haifa who had surreptitiously visited me a few weeks ago, stuck on top of the words 'All my love from Haifa' written in black ink made from a combination of beer and coffee (later, I had covered up the hair and the writing with a picture of my father, in case my previous affair was discovered by a new woman who had promised to pay me a visit); *my* dirty plates (My God! Did she think I would not recognise my own plates, covered with my dried-up leftovers?); *my* old stale bread and jam on the table; *my* horrible mattress which has never seen daylight; *my* worn out carpet that I found in the bin near the house of an important government official; *my* dirty curtains that a friend (who actually hates me) gave me when he stole a better quality set of curtains from a carpet shop (left open when the owner went to pray); the half empty bottles of beer that *my* guests had left before they fled to their own towns, afraid of the increasingly bad security situation in this city that kills itself little by little every day.

But here was this woman and her knife, her tender, white, unruly, breasts that were largely covered by her crossed arms, her mobile phone in front of me, and the smell of lemon coming through the window which hung heavy over everything in my room – but, oh God, was it really my room?

'Please,' I said to her, 'if you are running away from someone, I am happy to let you stay in my house. But if you are trying to claim this is your house and that I have broken in, you're mad. No-one will believe it. I could call the police right now and they would tell you whose house this is. I have a lease that identifies me as the tenant.'

'The police?' she replied. 'You break into my house in the middle of the night and talk to me about the police? I'm the one who should be calling the police. I have a lease with my husband's name written on it very clearly. Everything here belongs to me or my husband. Look at these pictures of my husband's dead friends: Hussein who was killed in 1996 during the events at the Western Wall Tunnel, Khalil who died of cancer in Amman, Ezzat who committed suicide – shot himself after a failed love affair. Just look at my wardrobe. Do you have a wife? If not, why is it full of women's clothes? I beg you. I'm afraid of the scandal. My husband works as a security guard at a minister's house and his shift ends in half an hour. Please leave.'

I moved towards my cupboard and she bristled with fear, worried that I was going to attack her. But I reassured her with a quick motion of my hand. I told her: 'Wait one second and I will prove to you that I'm right.' I opened the first draw and took out my passport.

'Read the name on this passport.'

She reached out her hand, opened it up, and read out the name in a clear voice: 'Ayman Sharif.'

I lost it.

'Who are you? What do you want from me? This is my passport, and my name is Ziad Khadash.'

I snatched the passport out of her hand and my whole body was shaking. I put my finger under my name and asked her: 'Are you blind? Spell it out with me: Z–I–A–D K–H–A–D–A–S–H.'

She let out a pained, shattering scream that shook the walls of the room. 'You're the crazy one. You're cruel too – and illiterate! For God's sake, get out of here. My husband is on his way home. How will I convince him that you just got lost and turned up at the wrong house? Should I tell him that you are stupid or will I have to say you are mentally ill?'

'Where do you want me to go?' I responded to her. 'This is my house; I don't have another one. The women's clothes belong to my girlfriends who come and visit me then leave behind some items of clothing as reminders, temporary goodbyes, or final farewells. Do you understand?'

She bent over, her eyes darkened, and the knife fell to the floor along with her mobile phone. Her breasts fell out, hanging in the air what seemed like an eternity, innocent as a child and confused as a butterfly. Then, she let her body fall. She had fainted; she was unable to talk and was having difficulty breathing. I moved towards her.

'Please, calm down. You can leave in peace or you can stay here tonight, if you want. Don't worry, I know you need someone to take you in; I can tell that you are on the run from your family or your husband. Trust me. You are a lucky woman. I am a writer, so I understand how much women suffer in this country and I want to help out however I can. Tell me your story; I'm listening.'

'My God! What's happening to me? You're torturing me. I don't know who you are or what you want but I am not on the run from anyone. I am in my house, that my husband and I rented four years ago from Abu Elias and Umm Elias. All the neighbours know me and they know my husband too – the man who I am waiting for and who is going to come in at any moment and kill me with that knife because he will think I have been cheating on him.'

This woman was strange and probably dangerous. There was clearly some kind of a conspiracy against me but I didn't know who started it. I rented this house from Abu Elias exactly four years ago. How did this woman know everything about me? I had no idea what to do next. Should I leave? Should I call the police? Should I go get the landlord? Should I force this woman to get out of my house? Should I leave and go to a friend's house, sleep on it for a night and figure out what to do in the morning? Or should I just go to sleep on my sofa? I was so tired I could have just passed out into a deep sleep and not even noticed she was here.

I sat down on the plastic chair by the door, with my head in my hands like a wayfaring traveller begging for food or somewhere to sleep for a while. The woman started crying in front of me like a child. Then suddenly, I noticed myself crying too – more than I had ever cried in my life before. It was strange; I had no reason to cry this much. I was weeping for the whole forty years of my life, for everything that I had lost and would never get back. The loss of this house became emblematic of all my life's losses. Oh God, would this night never end?

'I'm going to be killed tonight,' she wept. 'Oh God, my throat will be slit from ear to ear.'

'You're not going to be killed, lady. Because I'm going to leave now. I'll come back tomorrow to shave and change my clothes. Then I'll go to my school. But right now, I'm going to sleep at my friend's house. Please, you have to admit what is going on. Find some other house, some other game, and some other victim. I know what you're up to.'

'You're not going to come back tomorrow because the police are coming to arrest you now.' As she dialled the number for the emergency services, she started to breathe heavily, beseeching God to delay her husband's return just a little.

The chubby policeman pursed his lips in surprise as he read the name on the rental contract: Samir Khaled.

The woman shouted at the top of her voice: 'My lord! You too, officer? Have mercy, please! My husband is coming to kill me. Who is this Samir Khaled? My husband is Ayman Sharif!' She extended in the last syllable of 'Sharif' hysterically.

I spelled out my name as it was on the contract for the policeman, but he pushed me away with his two large hands, saying: 'You don't need to teach me to read, you miserable little man!'

At that very moment, the landlord, Abu Elias came in, disturbed by our loud argument. He gave all three people in the room a bemused look, as if this was the first time he had seen any of us.

The woman, jumping up and down in front of us like a madwoman, shouted with a mix of joy and anxiety: 'I knew that God would never abandon me to you two and your schemes.' She was acting like she had just escaped a death sentence. 'Abu Elias, brother, tell them who I am. Aren't I the wife of Ayman Sharif, who rented this house from you four years ago? Don't we all spend almost every evening together, staying up late and sitting in the back garden? Didn't you say you'd lower our rent because salaries had been suspended? Didn't you and Umm Elias talk to us just yesterday, telling us that we should have a child? Didn't Umm Elias bring us a bowl of mahalabia[1] when she heard that my husband was dying to eat the perfect mahalabia?'

Abu Elias looked at her suspiciously and angrily. As he cast the same look over me and the policeman, his breathing and the movement of his face and eyes became threatening.

'I'm sick of lying women and their tricks, claiming that they are persecuted, or poor, or sick, or on the run. Just the other week an old woman knocked on my door claiming that she had been sent by my sick brother in Brazil, saying that she wanted me to give her some money for medical treatment and that my brother had told her to come to me. This old scammer didn't realise that my brother has been dead and in his grave for two years. And you, are you one of these women? What are you doing in the house I rent out to Fadi, the student? Are you his girlfriend? The poor boy has gone to Jenin. His mother is very ill, and he left in such a hurry that he forgot to lock the door. He called me telling me to lock it for him, so I was surprised to hear voices in here.'

The woman was crying so loudly that she had woken the neighbours, who were now gathering outside my house – was it even my house? – confused by the commotion.

'And who are you?' said Abu Elias stabbing his finger at me. I couldn't get a single word out to answer him. I had lost, but I wasn't sure who the winner was in this strange game. All I knew was that this was my house. I moved towards the door, taking one last look at the woman. She was trying to stand, so I took her by the hand and helped her get up. She was crying silently and whispering to herself, 'He'll murder me… he'll murder me.'

I was dizzy and had no idea what was going on. I couldn't even think. So, we went out together, walking toward Rukab Street. Ramallah was sleeping and we did not exchange a single word. We parted just outside the Ramallah Café and she turned down al-Ahliyya College Street. I lit a cigarette and stood there smoking and waiting.

Note

1. A milk pudding usually also consisting of rice, sugar, and rice flour.

A Garden that Drinks Only from the Sky

Liana Badr

Translated by Alexander Hong

SHE STILL REMEMBERS HER first visit there, exactly five years ago.

She woke up happy and alert, her thoughts consumed by instructions the *weili*[1] had given her in a dream. He had a handsome face, complete with stately, white beard. He gestured towards the south, a rosary of glinting gold beads entwined around the long fingers extending from his palm.

'Go, my child, to the Sanctuary of Abraham in Al-Khalil,' he said and with a final steely-eyed glance, disappeared.

To the Cave of the Patriarchs, then. The neighbourhood women often spoke of all those honoured there, though she herself had never been. Following the sheikh's bidding in the dream, however, she resolved to carry out his wish.

Following her dawn prayers, she prepared for the day. She placed a ball of labneh in a muslin cloth bag which had hung from the kitchen tap. In a handkerchief, she bundled up two tangerines and a slice of bread spread with labneh she had made herself from the milk she had delivered every other day. God only knows what those plastic yoghurt cartons at the grocers contained, she thought; probably the only pure thing in them was water.

In her wicker lunchbox, she also placed a small bottle of water. She left the house dressed in traditional country clothes: a white thawb with red embroidery depicting cypress branches. Against the biting, early morning cold that was already numbing her face, she wrapped her scarf tightly around her as she made her way to the bus station.

Though she had never been to Al-Khalil before, she would visit Ibrahim, Father of the Prophets, and beseech him for rainfall to water her patch of land at the edge of town. This allotment of hers had been parched by a merciless dry season. On her last visit, it was a complete mess. She found rocks strewn about, as if an earthquake had struck in the middle of the night, and saw how shrivelled and dry the leaves and branches of all the fruit trees were.

If the skies didn't open their floodgates soon, there would be no red prune jam to make for the seasons ahead. Breakfasts would be devoid of this lustrous preserve, whose sweetness would counterpoint the tartness of the Nablusi cheese and homemade bread, in that daily awakening of the taste buds. Without rain, there would also be no guarantee of figs, fuzzy green almonds, or the plump olives she packed so tightly in brine. None of this would be ready to help her face the long winter and absurdly high living costs ahead.

She would go and beseech God, just as dozens of the women in her neighbourhood did every time they visited *her*, complaining and grumbling until she agreed to divine their fortunes from her coffee cups. Griping about men, children, or mother-in-laws, these women envied her foresight, her ability to pierce the veil between this world and the other. And yet to them, she also was just a 'little girl' whom no one would ever marry. Her stature was so diminutive in fact that it did indeed deter suitors, despite her beautiful almond eyes.

She was raised by her mother and stayed on in the same house with her after her brothers had left. But her first priority was taking care of that piece of land on the western edge of Ramallah. Staying with her mother brought no benefits beyond the pleasure of reading fortunes in the fine lines of granules left at the bottom of people's cups. The women would visit in the morning to drink cardamom coffee, showering her with compliments about her unusual skills. To her, though, it was no more than a question of interpreting sinuous brown marks. She knew why they believed so strongly in her supposed God-given abilities. Behind her back, the women would call her a midget, and assume she had dwarfism.

What drew most attention to her shortness, though, was how tall her mother was by comparison. In advanced age, her mother was nearly blind, but standing next to her daughter, the two of them looked like the Arabic number – ١٠ – the tall trunk of a one next to the tiny dot of a zero.

She always greeted the local women with an easy smile and gentle banter, leaving them ignorant of the anxiety she kept just beneath the surface. She secretly scoffed at them for thinking she had made some sort of pact with the king of the Djinn. The women assumed this because her clear almond eyes were of two different colours – neither of them exactly green, grey or blue. Along with her small size, this heterochromia was thought to be another sign of her affinity with the djinn.

She rose above it all. Even those things the Occupation brought, like higher prices and the destruction of fields decades old, whose crops protected the earth from erosion. Only small fragments of land not yet swept up in the settlers' plans remained of the old country. Countless olive trees had died because settlers, or their soldiers, had seized them and then neglected them.

Having confided in God about her fears, she resolved to go to Ibrahim of Al-Khalil, Father of the Prophets, and petition him about her great misfortune. Surely, God, the Beneficent, would provide a little rain for her land at the edge of the city!

On the bus, she ate all but the slice of bread spread with cheese. She had also remembered to bring a sesame-laced Al-Quds ka'ak[2] and some baked eggs. If she got to Al-Khalil late, she wanted to have a good breakfast. Besides the smell of diesel wafting through the bus and making her cough and feel queasy, the journey was easy. It didn't take long and she actually arrived early, after which she quickly made her way to the site of the Prophet's Cave.

Calling upon God and beseeching him, she ascended many steps. As she headed inside, she recited private prayers under her breath, asking for mercy upon the souls of all the martyrs who were murdered here once by a fundamentalist Israeli settler.[3] It was a massacre that happened during the holy month of Ramadan in the middle of prayers inside the Sanctuary of Abraham.

She was in the section of Ibrahim's Sanctuary reserved for Muslims. After the settler had done his deed, the Israeli army divided the entire complex into two halves, one of which only settlers could enter, the other only Palestinians. She rushed to the prayer room to get there before the crowds.

As she was finishing her last prostration, and sitting back up, without warning, she was suddenly struck by something – a heavy solid mass.

She had never imagined what a soldier's boot would feel like, kicking her square in the back of the head, but it came with such force she tumbled forwards. She hit the floor and the room span. Instinctively, she curled up into a ball and tucked her head in. When her vision settled, the butt of a large rifle came into focus hovering above her head. Coming to her senses slowly, she reached down to cover her calves where her thawb had scrunched up.

The blue-eyed solder was jeering at her. Unable to do much else, she remained perfectly still for a moment. Then, sitting up slowly, she composed herself and straightened out the sides of her thawb. The blow had silenced her and she continued to say nothing. She wondered if this was some prelude to something worse, if the soldier would carry out the kind of massacre that settler had, leaving no trace of some victims for anyone to mourn.

She couldn't tell him off, but neither could she ignore him. Instead she smoothed out the rest of her clothes, adjusting the white cloth covering her head. But as she tried to stand, she was seized by a pain radiating from the front of her head. The soldier was unremorseful, his face twisted into a harsh rictus. He retreated from view and an old Al-Khalili woman emerged wearing a traditional Dara'a dress.

'In the name of God, my sister. Everything is alright. The deranged ones have gone. Come with me, and rest for a moment.'

Gradually, she became aware of the woman helping her stand up and straightening her out. The old woman introduced herself as Umm Abdullah and invited her back to her house to recover.

Slowly they made their way up a hill to an old, thick-walled house, overlooking the Sanctuary of Ibrahim. The first room they entered had high ceilings and a large iron-framed window set in a wide, carpeted alcove. Umm Abdullah told her to rest herself there.

She made herself comfortable between the neatly arranged ornate flowerpots hanging from the wrought-iron window frame, caressed now and then, by the gently rustling leaves dangling from them. Umm Abdullah pointed beyond her to the resting place of Ibrahim and said, 'No one can get to the Prophet. Every other day, it's absolute bedlam as they attack us. But no one can get to him.'

Then, more amicably, she asked, 'And what do we have the pleasure of calling you, my dear?'

The guest said, 'Your obedient servant, Najah...' and then she hesitated, thinking to herself – *Are you going to call me a midget behind my back, like all the others do?* – then continued, '...from the house of Abu 'Azam, in Al-Bireh.'

'Oh, blessed be!' Umm Abdullah exclaimed, going on to try and connect the origins of their two families through distant relatives. She told Najah to make herself at home and made her move the sheepskin floor-cushions, in front of the copper-coloured bench embedded in the wall. Najah related all that had happened since arriving in Al-Khalil earlier that morning, detailing her preparation and her vow to stand before the prophet Ibrahim in the hope of quenching the thirst of her drought-stricken patch of land. Umm Abdullah resolved to make them both dinner that evening and suggested Najah daub some sesame oil on her bruises. She ignored her objections and even invited her to stay the night.

Before long it was afternoon. Umm Abdullah needed to run some errands, and while she waited for her to return Najah began to admire the Al-Naseem plant delicately ascending one of sides of the thick iron window frame. As she studied it, a knock came from the door, and on opening it she then found herself face-to-face with a male stranger, who promptly said, 'With your consent...'

This startled Najah, as she had not prepared herself for the presence of an unrelated male. At this moment, Umm Abdullah rushed into the room behind him and introduced her son, Abdullah, who was carrying her groceries for her. He put them down quickly and left.

Najah had barely glanced at him before his mother began regaling her with tales of his miraculous survival of a battle in Lebanon. She did not get the full story until he returned that evening. They stayed up late into the night, each reclined on long-floor cushions around a bowl of nuts Abdullah brought.

Savouring the rich tea, Abdullah roamed from one story to another. Accompanied by the cracking of almond shells and Sudanese peanuts, Abdullah carried on with his narration as if he were talking about someone else. Whenever he moved from one chapter to another, he would gaze intently, tenderly, at Najah with small, dark brown eyes.

Abdullah had been a regular private among the Palestinian fedayeen in Lebanon and had returned to Al-Khalil a few years ago. In Sayda, during the Israeli army's 1982 invasion of southern Lebanon, he was injured and his compatriots had thought him martyred. With the blood still spurting out of him, he crawled to the corner of a town square and hid himself among the bodies of the fallen. He passed out and was left there for a day and night as the fedayeen withdrew. Nurses eventually discovered him unconscious between stiffened corpses in a hospital morgue, his skin covered in dried blood. He had survived.

Umm Abdullah chortled. With her gold teeth glinting, her wrinkled cheeks shining, and her eyes ablaze, the sap of youth seemed to flow in her again and she declared, 'We still have him!'

For the first time in her life, Najah's heart pounded against her chest. This was a resistance fighter who had offered his life, and been brought back from the dead by God. She lifted her left hand to her heart and imagined herself for a moment standing down there in the Prophet's Sanctuary. If she didn't go down to Ibrahim's Tomb the very next day and recite prayers of thanks for all God's glorious and sublime bounty, her vow to the *weili* would be broken. But she could not escape her fear. Perhaps the same, mocking soldier would still be there.

But the joy she felt in her bosom hearing Abdullah's story of survival gave her strength. Tomorrow, it would help her decide if she could return once again and fulfil her vow.

In the end, Najah postponed her pilgrimage to Ibrahim's tomb and returned to Ramallah early the following morning. It was not just out of fear of the soldier, but concern that her further absence would alarm her elderly mother. She planned to return the next week, after she had fully recovered.

Najah returned to Al-Khalil many times in the weeks that followed, becoming almost like a member of Umm Abdullah's family. She came to know the obstacles Abdullah faced in trying to bring in his own wife and children back into the country, how they had been waiting for years for 'reunification' documents, as so many other families had. Anyone without official birth certificates and travel documents were unable to receive such documents. In Abdullah's case, his wife and children were forced to leave the Ain Al-Hilweh camp[4] during the last invasion of Lebanon, losing their papers in the process.

Najah cherished these visits. With each trip, her desire to hear more of Abdullah's story grew. In turn, she would tell them about her allotment, a grove planted with fig trees, hawthorn berries, cashew, and native plums. She would also tell them how militarised bulldozers were, little by little, approaching a particular mound close to the land. These huge machines were clearing away ground for a settler-only road that would connect their settlements to a string of security outposts and watch towers.

Najah swallowed before saying, 'Right now, they're still a good distance away. I still have hope.'

Sometimes, Abdullah spoke to her with his head cocked to one side as if slightly unhinged. 'Our houses and land are all gone,' he would say, 'nothing remains of them. Nothing but this room.'

Najah had come back a week after the first trip, then the week after that and so on. Stories gave way to more stories, and all the while Abdullah gazed at her with those small affectionate brown eyes. Was he flirting with her?

Agh – Najah thought to herself – *for the first time in your life, someone looks upon you without that oh-so-familiar expression of disdain or contempt, without thinking you're some kind of freak.*

They continued to talk, transfixed with each other.

On one occasion, Najah challenged him on his version of an incident in the war. He mocked her in return, riling her up, and she felt a little light-headed. Her eyes brimmed with tears and her heart raced. It was a feeling she couldn't explain, let alone share with anyone.

Oh, Abdullah, who kept confessing how much he enjoyed her company, had caught her hands in his and pulled them to his face. Najah would never forget his scent in that intimate moment. Among all the many memories of this time, she remembered the sensation of her whole body shuddering like the glow of a fire in a wintery storm.

He wanted Najah to leave her mother and marry him, so they could be together. But she already knew what would happen. Her family would not accept a husband like this. She didn't even dare tell them why she was visiting Al-Khalil so often, in case they stopped her going again. She explained her visits by saying it was for the sake of the land and the dryness afflicting it. Month after month the rain refused to come and slake its thirst, not even in winter.

When at last she convinced herself that Abdullah's family would never be allowed to return, Najah prepared herself to give him her consent. As soon as she resolved to do this, though, Abdullah's efforts finally paid off and his family received their reunification documents. His wife, four sons, and a small daughter would all be rejoining him soon, although not yet because of the eruption of the Second Intifada. Their entry would have to wait until the clashes subsided.

Najah stopped visiting. She went over all her reasons, reciting them one by one, before calling Abdullah on his mobile. It was a phone he carried with at all times, clipped to his belt as if physically attached to it. Considerate as ever, he asked her first about her allotment. Listening to his voice, she began to imagine the two of them standing side-by-side, the golden light slanting towards them, giving the orchard-covered hillsides around Al-Khalil an unforgettable colour.

Najah told him she was busy campaigning with other land owners against confiscation. She told him about the march she had organised, and how they had fled when soldiers began showering protestors with tear gas. Fear that day had gripped her like a steel corset, and she fully expected to have to run, next, from a round of rubber-coated steel bullets. The tear gas stung her throat and made her chest feel like it was being scraped from the inside by sharp rocks.

Najah did not tell Abdullah how afraid she was.

She was ashamed of confessing to that fear, even as the bulldozers started closing in on her land.

The occupying army shut down all the checkpoints. There were more marches and demonstrations, more stone throwing, even kids started risking their lives in the crosshairs of their rifle scopes.

She arrived one day to the near side of her land, finding it cordoned off by new barbed wire. It was to become the shoulder of a settler road that had already opened for traffic, thanks to the clearing work of bulldozers specially fitted with gun turrets. The land adjacent to the roads was now confiscated, even though the owners had yet to receive any notification of the seizure.

Every evening, now, as she finishes the housework, Najah reminisces about that first trip to Al-Khalil. After dinner, once her mother has fallen asleep, she lays down on the sofa-bed.

And every night, she reaches under the mattress to take

out a cutting from a local newspaper, folded into small squares.

She opens out the article, and from among its creases emerges a picture of Umm Abdullah leaning over the body of her only son, her face convulsed in grief, her eyes wet with tears. And every evening, Najah sobs for not being able to visit her because of the IDF's occupation of Ramallah. She gazes at the small caption beneath the photograph explaining how the army mistakenly shot at a civilian who had stopped in front of a shop, how he had been collecting empty cooking gas canisters from houses around the old city, near Tel Rumeida, and the soldiers had taken him to be a terrorist threat.

Every night she looks at the picture and thinks of the land she cannot return to and whether water from the winter sky will fall on it.

Notes

1. Weili – a blessed or revered sheikh or holy man.

2. Ka'ak – a type of bread similar to a dry and hardened biscuit, usually ring-shaped.

3. On 25 February, 1994, a Brooklyn-born settler (and former IDF soldier), Baruch Goldstein, walked into the Hall of Isaac, where some 800 Muslims were at prayer, dressed in full IDF uniform (therefore going in unstopped by guards), waited until *sujūd*, the part of the prayer where worshippers prostrate themselves with their heads on the floor, then threw a grenade into the middle of the hall, and opened fire, unloading 140 rounds of ammunition from a IMI Galil assault rifle, killing 29 people and wounding another 125, among them many children. It transpired that a year before he had poured acid over the floor of the mosque, and assaulted six worshippers. A letter had been written to then Prime Minister of Israel, Yitzhak Rabin, by the Muslim authorities 'regarding the dangers' of Goldstein and asking for action to be taken to prevent daily violations of the mosque. Despite this, and Shin Bet (internal security) agents knowing about other threats he'd made, no action had ever been taken.

4. The largest Palestinian refugee camp in Lebanon, originally housing over 70,000 Palestinian refugees, but swelling to nearly 120,000, as a result of an influx of Syrian refugees since 2011.

The Horse's Wife

Ahlam Bsharat

Translated by Emre Bennett

I AM SPEAKING AS the wife of a horse!

I don't neigh. I speak normally. But what is strange is that I understand his neighs.

For years now I have been saying, 'Any man can walk away from a woman's life.' A phrase that represents the lives of every woman I've known. I also know that although any woman can exit a man's life, she can't easily pull away like a thread from a ball of a yarn. Instead she needs to be surgically removed like an organ. Men can leave suddenly, in one big push as if they were merely ghosts or shadows. Whereas only about one in seven women can completely free themselves of their man, like day from night. I don't know if anyone has published research on this – I certainly haven't. Sometimes research isn't necessary; it simply consolidates already known facts. And sometimes, it can even do damage, consolidating people's fears, and creating rules to live by – theories for life if you will – creating the illusion that life is just a matter of problems and solutions. I don't know why this isn't widely recognised, or why many of the world's academic institutes and research centres don't just call it a day. As for me, I like to call myself the only woman that is loved by a horse.

I can't raise my voice right now or tap away at my keyboard as I am not sure of the capabilities of this horse who became my husband just five days ago. He says that our relationship may have started in another life. I can't remember what my soul previously inhabited, where his soul was or what form I took, but he understands me. Every time his heart beats, he is reminded that I am in it. Each beat informs him that it will forever resonate with my name. Perhaps my name is engraved in the walls of those sanguine chambers in paintings that only anthropologists would be able to decipher. If you knew that a horse has five hearts – one in each hoof and one in its chest – you would understand the significance of this. Especially given that horses always need to be running which keeps their hearts beating in time with their hooves – in this way my name is scattered with the wind down each travelled road.

Is there a theory for that?

The doorbell rang, eventually prompting me to get up as it chimed for a second and third time. I have already paid the residence committee 100 shekels for the cleaning, I haven't dropped any plant material from the parapet recently – as I did last spring when I pruned my flowers, instantly bringing two neighbours to my door. I knew I must have caused some catastrophe, seeing them standing there with plant trimmings coming out of their ears, then stepping back and pointing over the parapet down to a washing line hung on the first-floor balcony. There was soil covering children's jeans, skirts, shorts and a duvet cover hung in the corner.

But I wasn't expecting anyone today. If I were, then I would certainly know that I had an appointment. Having said that, since becoming forgetful and relying on vitamin B-12 pills, I have started doubting myself; so I got up. 'Maybe I am waiting for someone and I forgot,' I said to myself as I headed to the door.

Of course, it was the horse. If I hadn't mentioned in the first sentence that I was the horse's wife, you would now be as surprised as I was to find a horse at my door.

I don't want to describe to you my disbelief at this point, as I've previously made the issue normal. As if it is something that often occurs in Ramallah; horses knocking on flat doors. I also don't want to exaggerate anything as I know we authors often write simply to elicit sympathy of any kind.

It bites me too sometimes, this temptation. It's really just a result of readers being so far away and so dispersed in their houses in different cities across the globe. There is no way of seeing how and when a reader is being affected by one of my books, or how many are reading it, or indeed whether I will continue writing or become completely forgotten in time. But still, I'll continue this narrative, taking you through the events and elucidating the fiction that may actually be real, though I insist on calling it fiction. To express this in a purely classical way: fiction is the house I live in or, if I wanted to draw a tear from a sensitive reader, I would say 'Your eyes are my house, continue to read what I write.'

'What is this horse doing at my doorstep?' I said out loud.

'I came as you requested,' he said.

'Me?' I replied in astonishment. I couldn't tell whether it was the reply or the fact that I was standing in front of a talking horse who had just rang my bell that shocked me.

'Did you ring the bell with your hoof?'

'That is not why we're here.' His reply almost drove me crazy, controlling the conversation as if he had something to say.

'I *do* have something to say,' he interrupted, 'I wouldn't have come if I didn't.'

'How did you hear me?'

'I came *because* I heard you,' he replied. 'I heard the call of your heart that beats with its hoof.'

'Oh God,' I said to myself. There is no way to describe what it is like when someone who creates fiction is faced with it suddenly becoming reality.

'I *am* real.'

'Who told you? I think I prefer fiction to remain fiction.'

'Now that's not true.'

'Who are you to decide what I want?'

'I am your husband, and also I am not deciding, I am persuading you otherwise.'

'What are you saying?'

I almost lost it. Okay, so you don't sympathise with me. For some reason, these days, I feel quite alone and without readers who sympathise or pity me or even support my right to imagine.

'I said that I was your husband and I don't want you to be alone.'

'Who told you that I don't like being alone? Who told you? Then... Then look.' I stretched out my hand to point to his private parts. 'You are a horse. A high horse. And your penis... Look... and your hooves. And I am fragile and not very horny... and I'm slow, lazy and I can't take care of anything but a few plants.'

'I know everything about you.'

'How do you know everything about me?!' I started to get annoyed.

'Because I heard you.'

It was not appropriate to ask him what or how he heard. He would end up coming off better than me, with his calm, eloquent replies to all my crappy questions. During creative writing workshops, I would repeatedly tell my students that developing dialogue in texts is a challenge – even more challenging if that dialogue is between a horse and a woman. As well as taking into account the differences in gender and cultural background, you also have to consider the vocal organs and the sounds they produce. On top of that you still have to create the context for the dialogue and decide whether it should resemble a real or obviously fantastical conversation. Then you have myriad other factors affecting discourse: its complexity, breadth, strength, any tension, and the lexical choices. Before you know it these creative writing sessions turn into battles about all kinds of things. So, let me start anew here:

'Listen here, horse! Yes it's true that I have watched you through my window day in, day out. After which, I placed you in my imagination where I would usually transform your patch of grass into a garden, or a pasture, or a park, and sometimes a stable. I created you! Now go! Return to my head. Unless you are real, in which case return to your owner! I want to end this conversation. I live alone in this house withdrawn from all forms of communication. I don't want to take up speed walking and I hate leaving the house. I don't want to confide in you my opinions on men, or what my type is, or whether I'm actually in love or not. If I wanted to reveal anything to anyone I would write it into fiction and let it be read by everyone. And as a woman writer, I should remain vigilant, in a society like ours, as our personal lives are always being conflated with our writing.'

'You won't need to worry about other people when I'm with you.'

I laughed loudly, unable to stop myself. I was leaning on the railing and he was pushed up against the rubber plant in the earthenware pot by the door as I spoke all this nonsense to him. I was fixated by the way he was leaning on my plant – any more and it would snap. I kept glancing over at the lift and the opposite flat's door. If anyone were to suddenly come out – which was more than possible – and find me here conversing with a horse, they would go crazy. They would run through the streets of Ramallah shouting 'There's a talking horse back there and the crazy woman speaking with him is my neighbour!'

He interrupted my train of thought saying: 'I told you not to worry about what others think when I am with you. You know it wouldn't change the reality of this city one bit if a woman married a horse.'

'Of course,' I snapped back. I didn't know why I was angry. Whether it was the voice of that character running through the streets without finding another writer to deter her while I was preoccupied here talking to a horse. Perhaps I was being exposed by this character right now, without my knowledge, being called crazy by them with each scream – if they are even screaming. Perhaps my secret had been discovered and they were telling the world that I was a horse's wife.

At that moment, I wished I was a ewe; perfectly disguised with a tail hanging from my rear and entirely encased in wool.

'Of course,' I said angrily as I imagined myself as a ewe. 'It's Ramallah, anything is possible. Every accusation here has the potential to define the city, the way all Arab cities are like their women; afflicted by every dishonour thrown at them. 'But I love Ramallah!' I shouted to snap out of these thoughts.

'I love it too,' said the horse affectionately in either a neigh or man's voice – I couldn't tell anymore, 'because I finally met you here.'

I almost fainted. Sometimes the reader must trust the writer even if they are writing something completely illogical. For writers themselves have their own dilemmas while they're writing, and no doubt get caught up in their own universes and become like a cat stuck up in a tree after its owner has taken the ladder from under it. This horse was previously just an entertainment. His presence helped me overcome my isolation here. I wanted to create a connection with anything outside that moved since I was trapped in my house after the government announced the city's lockdown rules. It is true that I was already waiting to sequester myself away before this happened with no need to socialise with others. People may not believe that I wished everyone's lives were contained behind their doors and now I have locked my life up behind my door after the ruler of my universe decided to take the ladder from against the whole world's tree.

Since 22nd March 2020, I have kept my door locked with the key still stuck in the keyhole while I have stood by the window trying to see life from the inside. That's when I saw the horse, this animal there grazing the grass with its thick lips. I didn't conceal the fact that I was becoming more and more obsessed with him each day and would be filled with joy each time I saw him come down to the area behind the flats. Perhaps I got attached to his presence. Yes that's it! I chose all that. I chose to slow things down. There's no need to rush the experience. I don't understand why we rush to judge those who make wrong decisions. It isn't research and the purpose of choosing isn't to come out with some theory. This is a particular case and what is particular about it is that I am the only one who chose to remain alone in a city teeming with the country's national institutions and the people who visit them. Then in my isolation, surrounded by the sun on three sides, I decided to look out of one particular window, having five to choose from, and happened across this horse in his fenced space.

'How many areas in Ramallah have a horse grazing in some grass leading to a woman growing accustomed to watching it during the lockdown?'

'Look,' he said, 'It wasn't coincidence, was it?' he continued. 'I have been waiting impatiently for this day.'

'Tell me that it was you that convinced the government to put the city in lockdown to safeguard people from the pandemic, and that it was you who spread the pandemic across the world from its original source, sending people into hiding, scared in their houses – just so that we'd be here together!'

'I don't want to scare you. Right now you are my wife, you are my shelter and refuge so don't tell anyone about this, not even your friends. I admit that I am part of a secret movement amongst the animals to revolt against humanity.'

Silence.

'You aren't like them.'

It started happening when I read something somewhere. I remember! I came up with it! I wrote in one of my diaries that I was watching a horse and he would end up ruling the world.

'You were right.'

'But it sounds too clichéd to be a valid idea. It doesn't even sound that creative. I say to my students during writing exercises that sometimes the purely realistic writing can feel like it's being dragged through the mud and that it would be better left more fantastical, and unrealistic. Like a flower that wilts once it has been picked or a romance that goes stale in the day-to-day of married life. It's the same with you; you were more beautiful when you were grazing grass with your thick lips in that abandoned space behind the flats which I gave four different names to. I used to watch you so affectionately.'

'And lustfully.'

'Okay, even if I did, you are now a real horse and I don't feel any attraction towards you, even if you are the leader of a revolution. You see, I never dreamt of becoming the heroine of my story. I am the writer who creates heroes and normal people; that is my propensity. You know what happens to the heroes nowadays? They waste away in silence.'

'And you know what happens to authors?'

'I don't want to open that can of worms. All I want is to end this conversation.'

'All I want is to whisk you away and take you to the forest, the river and into the poetry you write from your flat, from here, from inside your kitchen surrounded by your dishes, from on your sofa where you spend most the day.'

'I love my house even with it being in the residential area of the city close to thieves and drug peddlers. I think you know where I belong.'

'Of course I know. But I know you also love the mountains and plains.'

'The barren area behind this building is enough for me. In spring it becomes covered in grass. When I win an award for writing someday, I will buy some land on the outskirts of the city and build a wooden hut. I will buy a cow which I'll tie up near the door and a dog which I'll let come and go on its own.'

'You won't buy a horse?'

'I don't like horses, you know I like donkeys.'

'I know. It doesn't annoy me though. I know you will love me with time.'

The horse is currently in the bedroom, reclining on his back with his private parts facing up to the ceiling – in a flat the size of a dormitory: 110 square metres, including the balcony. Nestled on the east side of Ramallah, in Um al-Sharayit district, overlooking Qalandia Checkpoint. I give the bank opposite my house 700 dollars a month and after 21 years this apartment will be mine. Meanwhile Israel announces their annexation plan for Al-Aghwar and perhaps the rest of West Bank. There is a Tabu[1] for the house and it's also registered with the PA but I don't know who will have possession of it in the coming months or years. I don't think that the know-it-all horse has a clue what Israel has planned either. For now though, he's fast asleep without snoring the way men do. In fact, tomorrow I may write a story different to the one about him showing up at the door. Or I may act differently in it before he steps out of the elevator and rings the door with his hoof so that, by the time I get to the door, I open it to find no one there.

For now, I will leave him to sleep till the morning. Before I leave to meet my students for their creative writing course, though, I will write him a note the way they do in the movies:

'Hey, you helped me write "The Horse's Wife" yesterday. So, honestly, thank you. And before that you helped me through the isolation, despite not neighing once which was all I was waiting for. I left you a labneh sandwich in front of the microwave. I know you don't eat labneh and bread, but this is all I had when the idea of writing about you came to my mind. If I knew when I went into the city to buy paint and cardboard for today's art therapy class that I would think of writing about you, and that you would cooperate so much you would agree to be my husband, I would have brought you a watermelon or some mallow or barley. But I didn't know. Sorry.

'Leave the key by the rubber plant after locking the door but try not to lean on it and do not nibble any of the leaves.'

Note

1. Tabu comes from the Turkish word 'tap', meaning deed. It is part of Turkish property law, dating from the Ottoman era, and still used in many parts of the former Ottoman Empire, including Palestine. It requires an additional cost to have land or property registered under this system, and is separate to the Palestinian Authority's official land registry, but is meant to make property claims easier to defend. In the face of Israeli expropriation, however, even having your land registered with both the Turkish state and the Palestinian Authority often isn't enough.

Badia's Magic Water

Maya Abu Al-Hayat

Translated by Yasmine Seale

BADIA WALKS INTO RAMALLAH Hospital like she owns the place, unhurried, greeting everyone and taking in their greetings. Stories fly to meet her in a brew of caution, curiosity and fear. From Samira the receptionist (recently married, keen to please) she wants to know if the tranquillisers had their effect on her husband, who makes love to her like a bull. To Said the errand boy she promises a special treatment for his spine, which keeps him up at night. Now handsome young doctor Sami, whom the nurses like to stop and ask ridiculous questions about the weather and incurable diseases, is running towards her, reverently kissing her hand in the way of old movies. 'God keep you from harm,' she says with a laugh and asks about his mother, Sitt Fikriyya, who devoted her life to his becoming a doctor.

On Badia walks, swinging the orange carrier bag whose contents no one dares to ask about. The soft headscarf slips from her loose red bun as she totters down to the basement, fighting back a cheeky smile at the memory of the young doctor's kiss and repeating to herself, 'Keep you from harm.' She opens the door of the autopsy room with her blue-beaded key and swaps her coat for a white gown. Her mobile rings. It's Umm Salama, calling to say she has sent her a girl with psoriasis from Haifa. She had spotted her with her mother at the Khalaf perfume shop, told her that Badia would be able to cure her with her magic water, and directed her to where Badia worked. Badia is annoyed with Umm Salama (she tells this story to everyone) and worries that her workplace at Ramallah Hospital will turn into a shrine or, God forbid, a clinic. She was wrong to have told her about the water, and how it cleared her own hands of the eczema that had plagued her since Osama's death. Not to mention the woman who once snuck into the autopsy room to steal some of the magic water that had spilled off a girl's corpse, to use it for some spell or ritual, who, when Badia tried to remove her, had bent down to where the water pooled on the ground and tried to lick it up.

Samah, the nurse who makes the journey from Tammun every day, takes in the day's death schedule. The first corpse is a woman from Al-Bireh, near eighty. The second is a woman in her fifties who has to be prepared for transportation to Nablus. The third is a young woman of twenty who has spent three days in the morgue. A long day awaits, but Badia does not begin work before brewing a glass of tea with her special herbs and smoking a cigarette.

Badia does not like to wash younger women, the mothers least of all. She prefers the elderly, whose corpses everyone is in a hurry to get rid of and few will miss. Their daughters and the wives of their sons slip her a bit of money. It helps them shed their sense of helplessness in the face of the decline and inevitable death of an old mother, especially when the bedsores appear, pinking the bodies swollen from their long, motionless sleep and which, to the sons and daughters busy with their own lives, look like festering wounds. She would deal with the bodies of the two older women first, then work her way round to the young one.

Samah regards Badia with admiration and a little awe. She fascinates her friends with her strange stories. Her mother had warned her not to get too close to her in case it spoiled her chances of marriage. Did she want to stay single forever? The magic waters of the dead can do a lot. But in Badia's presence, Samah forgets this talk and goes on telling her about the road clogged with checkpoints, a preamble to the question she wants to put to her.

A month before, Badia had noticed a change in Samah, sensed she had a secret she could not tell anyone, not even her, Badia, to whom everyone opens their heart. Samah, as has become her habit, asks to leave work for an hour midway through her shift, a request she has made for the past month, ever since her return from a long holiday she claimed to have spent in her family's village home. If a person does not want to tell, Badia thinks, she will not ask.

Badia has finished with the first body: an easy task, everything prepared ahead of time and supervised by the wives of the dead woman's two sons. They stand, the wives, outside the autopsy room as Badia pours water on the plump body, reciting prayers. *Nothing crueller than a mother without daughters,* she thinks. A mother without daughters has no one to mourn her. One of the women had tucked fifty dollars into her palm before she began, and this makes her work with all her heart.

She places a clean towel between the legs, then pulls the right side of the body towards her and cleans it, then the left. Then comes the full ablution, and the wrapping of the head, then the whole body, in clean white cloth. She does not make the same effort with the second woman, who will likely be given a fresh shroud in Nablus by the women of her family.

Badia takes a break to smoke a cigarette, its taste unlike the one she smoked this morning. It is a waiting cigarette, smoked in the hope that Samah will come back. But Samah takes her time, and Badia is out of excuses to keep her from starting on the third corpse. Young bodies fill her with dread, not that she has seen many in her time at the hospital. Most of her young clients are girls, killed in stories of love and suspicion. Only two died of natural causes. The rest of the day, she knows, will be shadowed with gloom.

The workers place the body on a large slab in the middle of the room, covered with a blue hospital sheet. Three days in a fridge are enough to harden the softest body on earth. Badia is suddenly aware of a line of light from the window parting the darkness. The dust hanging in the room's air becomes visible. The voices of street vendors, mixed with the sounds of children on their lunch break at the nearby Qaddoura Camp girl school, filter down to the hospital basement. Badia lifts the sheet off the girl's face, revealing thick, wavy red hair which snakes down half her body.

The breasts hanging limply to the sides stop Badia, who understands at once that a baby's mouth has clamped itself around these teats: traces of redness and inflammation are still visible. The skin around the uterus and navel show that she had given birth not long before. Badia touches the skin and steps back. How could a body refrigerated for three days still be so warm and soft?

She rushes to the girl's file and reads. Twenty-nine years old, nurse, traces of poison in the blood. *They killed her.* the thought leaps to Badia's mind. They killed her. She clutches at her heart for a moment. She remembers it all as if it had just happened. Just seventeen when she met Osama, who trotted past their house in Al-Bireh on a white horse clad in black, she loved him straight away, and began to wait for him to leave the nearby mosque after evening prayer. The longer she waited for him to pass, the more she loved him, until the day she met him in a clothes shop in the Ramallah souq.

Only in that period did she come to understand the difference between Ramallah and Al-Bireh. The overlapping cities were divided by an imaginary line, existing nowhere but in the heads of their residents, but which became clear to her when Ramallah was chosen as their meeting place, far from the eyes of her mother's large family in Al-Bireh.

This was in the days of the First Intifada. They got engaged, entered university together, stole moments in rented cars on the roads between the city centre and the university in Birzeit. Those rendezvous were even sweeter than those at the house of her friend, who had not yet become Umm Salama. But Osama was killed in a flash, leaving her with a gift in her stomach. Had her mother not noticed what was happening, she herself would have been killed long ago.

Badia does not like to remember how she got out of that disaster. Her mother was clever enough to save her from death, but the foetus died after birth – boy or girl, her mother wouldn't say and she did not ask. She had felt delivered of a heavy burden when her mother told her it was dead and disappeared into the corridor of the private hospital in Jerusalem which she had snuck her into, with the help of a women's association specialised in protecting girls of this type.

A terrible void took the place of the disaster. A void from chest to womb that has stayed with her ever since. She has filled it with laughter, with solving the problems of her colleagues, washing the dead, this occupation she walked into after her mother died and she could not find a woman in the hospital to wash and shroud her. She took on the task herself, unafraid. It gave her a serenity she had not had before, a tremendous sense of calm. All of which made her leap to accept a job offer washing the dead. Since that day she has contented herself with a simple life spent observing the sorrows and joys of others.

The girl spread out on the slab before her moves between her hands so pliantly it strikes fear into Badia's heart. She pours water on her head and searches for marks of violence on her body, trying to reconstruct the girl's story. She goes back to the file: raised in an orphanage, born in October 1990. Badia's heart beats faster. She returns to the body and lifts the torso to wash the back. The girl's upper body relaxes into Badia's arms. Her head lies on Badia's left shoulder as if she were sleeping. The girl is calm, as if resting in her mother's embrace. Badia does not fight back the tears which begin to run down her cheek. With the girl's head still on her shoulder, she weeps. How sorry she is for this girl no one is waiting for. But she was a mother, that much was clear. Where is her child? Its father?

She rushes back to the file. Was she single? The child born out of wedlock? Was she poisoned to get rid of it? Back and forth between the body and the file, Badia approaches the head, cleans the nostrils, opens the mouth and passes her fingers between the lips as usual. When she turns the face to the right to clean the left ear, the eyelids fall open. The eyes are fixed on her. She knows this look. Very like the look she had given her mother on learning that her newborn was dead. A look of complete surrender, acceptance, release.

Samah enters the autopsy room. Badia comes back to her senses and tries to hold it together, but Samah is not paying attention. She is devastated, in tears. Badia leaves the body outstretched, covers it with a sheet again and turns to Samah, who is ready to tell her all. It was as Badia had suspected: Samah had given birth to a child out of wedlock. The man she loved had not promised to marry her, but she was convinced he would after the child was born. The baby was born in Ramallah, far from the eyes of her family – she told them she was there for a training workshop. Now she goes to breastfeed the child, which she leaves with his father, on her work breaks. But the man tried to suffocate the child with a pillow to get rid of it. Samah is at a loss, caught between wanting to protect her child from its father, and the fear that her family would find out.

Badia takes Samah's hand and tells her everything will be alright. But first she has to prepare this girl as well as she can. Samah relaxes at once, watching Badia perform the finest ceremony she has seen: out of her bag she takes Indian incense, a copper bowl, white cloth, Nablus soap, jasmine cologne, a tape of Abdul Basit reciting the Quran. This she slips into an old machine and his voice begins to chant the Sura of Women as she goes on washing the girl, with precise instructions for Samah to move her this way and that. She pours water on her pubis, on her thighs, then takes the copper bowl and begins to collect the water dripping off her body. She lays the bowl on the table with great reverence.

Then she dries the body well and wraps it in layer after layer of bright white cloth. From a distance, she sprays cologne around the body, then comes to sit quietly beside her, holds her to her chest and cries for a long time to the amazement of Samah, who did not expect to see powerful Badia behaving as a mother who has lost her child.

Her task completed, Badia asks Samah to tell the officials that the body is ready to go. She sits at her table, lights a cigarette. Then Badia asks Samah for the man's address, insisting that she would not approach him before he got in touch with her.

The following day, Badia slowly makes her way across Library Street, stopping to pick jasmine from the garden of the deserted house she passes on her daily walk to the hospital. At the Parliament Roundabout, she meets Umm Salama, who asks whether the girl with psoriasis had come to visit her. The answer is no: it seems the girl did not believe her when she told her that Badia would cure her with a bowl of magic water in which she washes the dead. Sorry as she is for the girl, Badia can do nothing for those who don't believe. Umm Salama dips her head in agreement. Samah is waiting anxiously at the door of the autopsy room and comes down on her with questions: what had she done? The father of her child had called the night before, begging her to marry him. Badia smiles, fishing from her bag the copper bowl. 'My magic water cures all sorts of ills,' she says. And she remembers the look on the young man's face as she wielded the bowl of magic water and told him that this water would scar his body with a permanent rash if he did not marry Samah. At the sound of the name Badia, the corpse washer from Ramallah Hospital about whom he had heard so much, he shook with terror and passed out.

Badia asks for the day's schedule without giving Samah the chance for further questions. No dead today: the schedule is blank. Badia sighs, removes her coat, puts on her clean white gown, and drinks the special tea of herbs she brewed herself.

Surda, Surda!
Ramallah, Ramallah!

Khaled Hourani

Translated by Andrew Leber

'ABD AL-GHAFFAR, NOW in his sixties, had regularly attended physiotherapy sessions ever since his right shoulder and hand had been seized by a sharp pain – the result of a slipped disc in his upper spine. The neurology specialist had prescribed the sessions after a long list of conventional medicines had failed to improve his condition. He'd chosen the treatment centre in the Mukhmas building, in downtown Ramallah.

It was the Second Intifada. The main road between Ramallah, Bir Zeit, and the nearby towns was closed by the occupation, its entire length marked by craters and earthen barriers. Taxis and vans took passengers from downtown only as far as the checkpoint – the Surda checkpoint, as it came to be known. From there, travellers had to walk on their own two feet across the divide – arriving covered in dust in the summer, caked in mud in the rainy winters.

The students and employees of Birzeit University were the heroes of this particular crossing,[1] weaving daily between a tangled mess of taxis, buses and private cars – to say nothing of the kiosks selling children's toys and knock-off clothing, the juice and coffee vendors, the beggars – at each end. New ways of life formed around the trenches and mounds. The place was filled with people hunting for the chance to work, and seizing any fleeting opportunities, at a time when most work and opportunity had vanished.

'Abd al-Ghaffar walked from Surda amid the scattered standoffs between the Israeli army and young Palestinian men (at the Manara roundabout in particular). Between the thrown stones, gunfire, tear gas canisters, screams, shouts and scuffles, life across the entire city was entirely upended.

The shops shut their doors as people ran back and forth in fear of the bullets, seeking refuge inside houses and apartment buildings. Amid all of this, 'Abd al-Ghaffar reached the clinic ready to battle through his treatment session in the Mukhmas building. He was one of only a handful who had managed to make it that day (through all the difficulties).

The specialist Osama al-Mughmari told them all: 'No reason to worry, you're all safe here! You're like family here – stay in the building until things calm down, and then we'll see how to get you home.'

One patient was from the village of Beit Rima, north of the aforementioned barricade (on the far outskirts of the Birzeit municipality). Once they took the bags of hot sand from off his feet, he got up and walked to the window that looked out over the battlefield.

The sounds of the bullets were deafening, mixing in with the honking of the cars and the hue and cry of drivers trying to get passengers into the waiting Ford taxis. The loudest of them was a driver next to the Arab Bank (Manara branch) calling out louder than a car horn – 'Surda! Surda! Surda!' – as if to rescue people from the hell of downtown as it fell to pieces.

No sooner had the patient from Beit Rima heard this call than he said, mostly to himself, 'That's it! I need to head home quickly before they close the checkpoint completely and the roads get snarled up. It'll be impossible to get home and I'll be stuck in Ramallah.'

He hurried out down the steps on his crutches and disappeared.

'Abd al-Ghaffar stayed in the clinic with patients who were mainly from the city (all seeking out normal treatments in the most abnormal of circumstances). They were waiting to see if their friend from Beit Rima would make it home successfully, mostly for their own reassurance. If somebody who lived that far away got there safe and sound, surely they could also get home once things calmed down?

They shoot each other looks filled with worry and anticipation. Then, after being gone for about half an hour, the patient from Beit Rima reappeared, hustling toward the clinic.

The clinic called out *'Welcome back!'* with once voice.

'What brought you back here?'

'What happened?'

'We just saw you hop into that Ford with the driver calling out, "Surda, Surda!"'

'Yes,' he said, 'I jumped in and we took off, and almost as soon as I'd paid the fare we arrived at the Surda checkpoint. But there were clashes, shouting, fierce standoffs just like the ones here on the roundabout, if not more! The only difference is that the taxis idling there shouted out the opposite direction – "Ramallah! Ramallah!" – as if they wanted to save people from the hell of the checkpoint! The very same driver who took me from downtown went from calling out "Surda! Surda!" to calling out "Ramallah! Ramallah!"'

'I jumped in the same taxi to come back, and here I am back in Ramallah in spite of everything. At least I made it here in one piece, after the tanks we ran into on the road next to the electrical company. We had to come all the way around through Al-Baloua.'

The questions rained down.

'What about lower Ramallah and Irsal Street?'

'What about Tira, can you still get there?'

Beitunia, Al-Bireh, Sateh Marhaba, Batan Al-Hawa, Al-Masayif, Al-Masyoun – no end of names echoed off the walls of the clinic, but the patient did not answer.

Instead, the man stretched himself out on the bed next to 'Abd al-Ghaffar and reached for the bags of hot sand. He piled them up over his entire body this time, snoring himself into a deep sleep.

Note

1. 'Heroes of the Crossing' historically refers to Egyptian forces crossing the line of Israeli fortifications along the Suez Canal in the October War of 1973.

The Sea

Anas Abu Rahma

Translated by Raphael Cohen

THE NIGHT BEFORE OUR trip to the swimming pool (the sea is a difficult proposition around here), we laid our mattresses along the corridor between the kitchen and the bathroom and practiced swimming. This was a 'dry-run' so we wouldn't drown in the pool but rather swim with confidence, flexing our muscles in front of tough kids from unknown towns and villages.

So many times I nearly split my head open climbing on to the sofa and diving headfirst onto the thin foam. I broke my glasses a few times too, and my mother would tell me off because she didn't have the money to buy me a new pair: 'I'm saving that money for the swimming trip – what with the tickets, lunch, trunks, and sun cream. You'll have to wait till the end of the week now before you can tell the difference between a snake and a hosepipe, four-eyes.'

You see, I had run to her one day, tearful and screaming. A long snake was climbing up from the bed of mint to the balcony of my room. 'Quick, go and kill it! And call the neighbours to help.'

Being terrified of long black snakes, she screamed and cried and rushed into the southern yard of the house wielding a mop handle. Still crying, she suddenly stopped and stared closely, then came back and slapped me across the face: 'Why aren't you wearing your glasses, you mutt? Why?'

Another time, I pulled the water out from under Yaman.

Crack. The blood from his head went all over the white tiles.

'Let me see. It's not too bad.'

'It hurts.'

'Just a little blood.'

'You crocodile!' my mother yelled. 'Stealing the sea from under your brother! You wanted to drown him on the tiles so that Reem would love you instead.'

Reem, the girl with blonde plaits, refused to play basketball with you in the alley, didn't she? – I chided myself – She claimed she had exams. Her teacher, Miss Widad had threatened her students with ten strokes of the rod across both hands if they scored less than 70% in maths. Yet fifteen minutes later you spotted her and Yaman playing with a skipping rope under the big sycamore tree. She was jumping and he was counting.

Whenever she bumped into you, out of breath on her way to somewhere else, you were quite certain that she searched your face for the small black mole that had sprouted above Yaman's left eye. When she failed to find it, she ran off to search the faces of other children scattered around the school playground and the classrooms.

You went up to the first floor and watched her meet Yaman coming out of the cafeteria with a bottle of ice-cold water. She took three Kinder chocolate bars out of her small bag, unwrapped one and brought it close to Yaman's mouth. The two remaining bars she slipped into his righthand jacket pocket. *Those bars are from her father's shop in the city,* you thought. Then they ran off to the back playground and you couldn't see them anymore.

You guessed that they were playing chase and splashing water over each other's hair: his cropped and hers blonde and tied in plaits.

'No, I swear I didn't think that.'

'So why did you pull the sea out from under Yaman then?'

'I felt sleepy. I wanted to go to bed on it.'

'You little liar.'

'Maybe.'

Tonight there was a power cut and the small Samsung fridge next to where I sleep, in hiding from the heat and the mosquitoes, had given up the ghost. I went swimming on the tiles between the kitchen and the balcony. Next to the burgundy TV-stand that my mother gave me two years ago as a graduation present, a blind crocodile attacked me. My arms flailed left and right with all the strength I could muster. I swam and swam to reach the balcony and jumped down onto the lemon tree, but the crocodile was still there in front of me. I kicked with my left leg against the tiles and changed direction. I swam and swam to reach the toilet, to save my skin by going down the waste pipe. But it was still lying in wait, mouth open to devour me. I tried and tried to flee. Whenever I made it to an exit, or what I thought was an exit, I found it waiting, mouth open to reveal white teeth as sharp as knife points. After an hour of swimming and crawling, I was completely exhausted. My limbs and joints seized up. The foul creature managed to grab my right hand after hemming me in between the cooker and the dining table. With its fangs, it dragged my hand down into its belly. I passed out when I saw the blood dripping like the sea from my severed limb.

Yaman had been sleeping at my house for a week. Reem had gone to Spain to complete her studies in medical physics, and he did not want to be on his own for three months in their large house. Next morning he was freaked out by all the blood on the tiles in my kitchen. He quickly pulled me out from under the dining table and despite examining my body, he could not find out where the blood had come from, so he took me to the city hospital.

He told me afterwards that as the doctor put his stethoscope over my heart I was screaming: 'Leave me a piece, you dog. Just one piece so I don't die.'

At the Qalandiya Checkpoint[1]

Ameer Hamad

Translated by Basma Ghalayini

HERE WE GO AGAIN. More waiting. Whether you come by car –
a fancy new model that races like the wind, or a metal tortoise
that splutters with smoke – or by foot – trudging along the
blackened path, sluiced with exhaust water spat out by the
terrifying lorries – it doesn't matter. Whoever you are, you'll
have to wait. You'll have to wait for so long the Qalandiya
checkpoint will start to chew away at you, the way a worried
father chews at his nails waiting for news of his son's death to
reach him from inside the operating room. Everyone is equal
in the eyes of the checkpoint.

They have flown in a team of anthropologists to create
something useful from the time wasted at this checkpoint. This
Norwegian study has shown that a human being is capable of
spending five years of his life on the toilet as a result of digesting
cod or salmon that's been smoked in the fumes of checkpoint
confrontations. In total, a human is capable of spending fifteen
years at the Qalandiya checkpoint. *A human, you say?*

Of course, even Scandinavian countries have checkpoints.
The most obvious example being the one my Norwegian
friend, Holst, told me about: the damn checkpoint at Oslo
Airport. There they will try to force you to read, study, listen to
music or do yoga for hours on end; someone has even opened
a pop-up café called 'Love at the Checkpoint'. But who would

attempt something so humanitarian at a checkpoint run by these Neanderthals?

It's a good thing you don't forget to breathe.

To be fair, this checkpoint has its advantages, most notably the fact that waiting here makes you experience time in its purest form. As Samuel Beckett famously observed, it doesn't get purer than this. Indeed, to quote Ronan McDonald in his *Cambridge Introduction*, Chapter 3, page 67, second sentence: 'Beckett wrote *Waiting for Godot* in the hours he spent at the Qalandiya checkpoint between 1948 and 1949 while he was studying Absurdist Literature at Birzeit University.'

As you wait, you can almost hear the ghostly sound of planes landing nearby at Jerusalem Airport – daily flights to our beloved Beirut; one-dinar flights to the proud and passionate Amman. And it's perfectly OK when, after hours of waiting your turn, you're obliged to let a woman go in front of you, to cross the border and catch one of the buses; it's also OK to stand there and watch a group of jet-setters complete the final stage of their journey of discovery, passing through the gate. When these things happen, you have two reasons to be happy: the satisfaction of being a gentleman, graciously giving up his place in the queue for a woman, and the joy of being one step closer to passing through yourself.

But just as you experience this double happiness, the mountain goes into labour and gives birth to a mouse, announcing on the speaker system: 'Aisle 3 is now closed. Please use Aisle 2.' It's OK, you tell yourself. There's no need to curse anything. No need to curse that woman who is now free and breathing the air that was meant for your lungs. Or the jet-setters taking your seat on the bus. It's OK because, after all, you'll soon be popping over to Beirut yourself for a quick lunch!

Of course, you should not for a second think that everyone is really equal. Not everyone is born like me. Indeed, here is my story, the story of a hero who overcame the Occupation's checkpoints and survived the intelligence services' dreaded detention containers. And let my story be a lesson for those who wish to learn, an example to all those who fight for freedom around the world, from Algeria to Cuba!

My mother gave birth to me at the Huwara checkpoint.[2] Her family were from Nablus and she was visiting them while she was nine months pregnant. My father, who was from Jerusalem, had long warned her about leaving the house at such a delicate stage. He hated her family as much as he hated the Occupation; they had put him through hell before eventually allowing him to marry my mother. People from Jerusalem don't have the best of reputations among those in the West Bank, you see.

When he heard that she was going into labour at the checkpoint, he came running out into the street in his underwear (yes, my father ran all the way from Jerusalem to Nablus), which only worsened the already bad reputation of his townsfolk. If I had not uttered my first word – 'Mah'som'[3] – then and there, he probably would have divorced her, he was so angry with her for disobeying him. From that day, my father thought of me as a blessed child and called me Salah ad-Din, after the great scourge of the Crusaders.

My primary school was on the left side of what would later be the Separation Wall, in the town of Al-Ram – I had to cross the old neighbourhood checkpoint on my way to it twice a day. My secondary school was on the right side of this line, where the wall would eventually be built when I was in seventh grade. Even before then, I had to cross checkpoint after checkpoint as if the line were following me, bending round to meet me again wherever I went. Having graduated from secondary school with flying colours, I enrolled at Birzeit University, even though Harvard begged me to join them – I had refused, you see. How could Salah ad-Din agree to emigrate to a land of colonisers?

I used to cross the checkpoint daily – I mean, the Qalandiya checkpoint. What you may not know is that when you cross, the soldier taps your ID number into his keyboard. The computer uses what they call in programming language, a counter function, which only accepts one type of variable: integers. The computer counts you in on its fingers, and when the number reaches a certain value, the soldier picks up his phone and receives orders to let you into the red room.

The red room is a small, narrow cell. In the old checkpoint, you would sit there on a chair resting comfortably for a couple of hours. But in the new one, they leave you standing there in the dark with only a spider on the wall to keep you company. You stand there like that for a few hours, then they let you go. But the computer doesn't forget. The camel that is this technology never forgets, and from then on every time you go through, they take you to the red room, and keep you waiting again, until they eventually feel sorry for you and give you a paper for an 'interview with Intelligence'. As your waiting goes on, you might yell at them: 'For heaven's sake, just let me meet the Captain! I want to become an informant!' But it doesn't help.

As for me, when the soldier first ordered me to enter the red room, I shouted and cursed as loud as I could, and the bulletproof glass cracked when I punched it: 'Who do you think you are, ordering me to come in! You sons of bitches!' The soldier immediately begged my forgiveness and sent me through to the Captain who arrived with his tail between his legs, kissing my hand apologetically.

He called himself 'Captain Ayman'. He spoke Arabic better than I could ever dream of, and was more up to date with news from my university than my fellow students were.

His smile wasn't that of a Captain of Intelligence, but a sales rep.

He led me into his office all the while apologising and begged me to grant him an informal interview, just a chat. He explained that it was just to reassure himself that he had done his job. The computer doesn't forget, you see, and it was better to lose your neck than lose your job. 'Isn't that what you say in Arabic?'

Seeing as I'm a kind man with a heart of gold, I agreed not to let him lose his job. I also saw this as an opportunity to exact a little retribution on Shabak[4] for all my friends and countrymen. I told myself I would turn this intelligence officer into a guerrilla and send him to Gaza to fight.

'What would you care to drink, Mr Salah?'

'Nothing. Just get this over with. I don't have the time.'

'Now, we can't have that! You Arabs are famous for your hospitality. If I came to your home, would you not offer me something to drink?

'No, I wouldn't. I'm not Arab. I'm Salah ad-Din, I'm Kurdish!'

'Suit yourself. Now please relax, sir, and tell me a little bit about yourself.'

'I refuse to tell you about my past, but I'm willing to tell you about my future and yours.'

'Please, go ahead, if you don't mind.'

'I am the one who will free Jerusalem, and bring the sun back to Haifa. I'm the one who will demolish this whole damn checkpoint and bulldoze it over your grandfathers' graves. I'm the one who will single-handedly bring back all the refugees, and deliver self-determination to the entire Arab world, I'm the one —'

'But you're Kurdish. Why are you bothered about the Arabs?'

'And you're Russian. What do you care about Palestine?'

'Sir, I'm taken by your honesty. Are you comfortable at university?'

'Very much so, thank you. I feel like I'm on a swing being gently swayed by a sea breeze.'

'You have an election coming up on the 20th, I believe. Who are you planning to vote for?'

'Islamic Jihad.'

'Aren't you the wit! I happen to know that Islamic Jihad consider elections to be haram.[5] Seriously, who are you voting for?'

'I won't vote, no one deserves my vote but me.'

'So, anyway... it says here that your father has seven children. How does he cope?'

'My father did that to himself. It's not my problem. Who told him to have seven children?'

'Well, don't you want pocket money? A little extra for outings and girls?'

'Come on now, don't be stupid! I'm a highly eligible suitor. No woman can reject me, no matter how great her... assets!'

'Not even a little bit of future financial security? You never know what might happen.'

'Damn you! Are you proposing that I become your eyes? Don't talk about things you don't understand. I am the future!'

'Why do you misunderstand, Mr Salah? I mean you can just tell me about the price of tomatoes and cucumbers in your neighbourhood, for instance. I am very worried about the Arab consumer. I hear that – poor thing – he can't make ends meet. We need to end this exploitation!'

'You remind me of that Korean – the Secretary-General.[6] Just stay out of the Arab's business and he'll be just fine.'

'What can I offer for you to work with us?'

That's when I felt all the martyrs' blood rise in my chest and a black river explode under my skin. I stood up in front of the Captain and began to sing – *'Fida'i...Fida'i'*[7] – the words echoing across the checkpoint's other containers. 'I want my country... I want my country from the river to the sea!' I bellowed.

You should have been there to see the tears roll down his cheeks. The guy started hyperventilating. 'Sir, it's not up to me. I swear, if it were up to me, I would give Palestine back to its people. I only do what I'm told.'

'"If it wasn't for you, they wouldn't be able to oppress us," as Ibn Taymiyyah[8] told his jailer.' I then gave the Captain an option: either go to Gaza as a fedayeen, or go back to St Petersburg, and since he hated the cold, and he didn't want to fall into a life of sin or drown in vodka, he chose Gaza. I heard that he was killed during Israel's last series of airstrikes.

And here I am again, passing through the electronic gate. Even the turnstile seems afraid of me now, by the sound of the strange squeaking noises it makes as it lets me through, faster than usual, as if some horse is dragging it open. And here is the gormless woman soldier tapping my ID number into her keyboard. She will be terrified once my profile pops up... Why is she not scared yet? She's picking up the phone. Is she calling a cardiologist?

She gestures for me to wait. She must be taking a liking to me – my handsome features sometimes undermine my status, you understand. She must want me to stay for as long as possible, that's why she's pretending to take an urgent phone call. OK, I'll wait, a woman is still a woman even if her nails are painted with blood...

Notes

1. One of the largest Israeli military checkpoints in the occupied West Bank. Not located on a border, but between Ramallah, Qalandiya Refugee Camp, and Al-Ram, it separates Ramallah residents from southern Palestinian towns and the northern Palestinian neighbourhoods of Jerusalem. The land beside this checkpoint was once Jerusalem Airport, operating between 1924 and 2001. Until it fell under Israeli occupation in 1967 (being fully annexed to Jerusalem in 1981) it hosted regular flights to Beirut and Amman, for Palestinians.

2. The Huwara checkpoint is a major IDF checkpoint at one of the four main exits of Nablus. Located south of the city, it was established in October 2000. The facility was named after the nearby village of Huwara.

3. *Mah'som* – Hebrew word for checkpoint, used in the colloquial Palestinian dialect.

4. Shabak – Israel's internal security service. Also known as 'Shin Bet' (a two-letter Hebrew abbreviation of 'Security Service').

5. Forbidden or proscribed by Islamic law.

6. A reference to Ban Ki-moon, then secretary-general of the UN.

7. *Fida'i...Fida'i...* – the opening words of the Palestinian National Anthem, meaning 'I give my life to you...'

8. Ibn Taymiyyah (1263–1328) was a controversial medieval Sunni Muslim theologian, logician, and reformer, whose iconoclastic views resulted in him being imprisoned several times.

About the Authors

Liana Badr is a novelist, story writer, journalist, and poet. Raised in Jericho, she obtained a BA in philosophy and psychology from the Beirut Arab University, but was not able to complete her MA due to the Lebanese Civil War. She has worked as a volunteer in various Palestinian women's organisations, and as an editor in the *Al Hurriyya* review cultural section. After 1982, she moved to Damascus, then Tunis, and Amman. She returned to Palestine in 1994. Since her first novel *A Compass for the Sunflower* (Women's Press), in 1979, she has since published three collection so of short stories (*Stories of Love and Pursuit, Golden Hell, I Want the Day*), a collection of novellas (*Balcony Over the Fakahani*), two further novels, a biography of the poet Fadwa Touqan and five children's books.

Ahlam Bsharat is a Palestinian writer who grew up in a village in Northern Palestine. She completed her Master's Degree in Arabic Literature at An-Najah National University in Nablus. Besides poetry, picture books, short stories, novels, and memoirs, she has written a number of television and radio scripts. Her books have received many awards and recommendations. *Ismee Alharakee Farasha* (*Code Name: Butterfly*) was included in the IBBY Honor List for 2012, a biennial selection of outstanding, recently published books from more than seventy countries. *Ismee Alharakee Farasha* and *Ashjaar lil-Naas al-Ghaa'ibeen* (*Trees for the Absentees*) were both runners up for the Etisalat Award For Children's Arabic Literature in 2013. *Code Name: Butterfly* was shortlisted for the UK-based Palestine Book Awards in 2017.

ABOUT THE CONTRIBUTORS

Ameer Hamad is a poet, short story writer and translator, who has published his work in numerous magazines and websites, including *Beirut Literature Magazine* and the New Arab website. He was born in Jerusalem in 1992, graduated from Birzeit University, with a major in Computer Science and is currently working on his first collection of short stories.

Maya Abu Al-Hayat (also editor) is a Beirut-born Palestinian novelist and poet living in Jerusalem. She has published two poetry books, numerous children's stories and three novels, including her latest *No One Knows His Blood Type* (Dar Al-Adab, 2013). She is the director of the Palestine Writing Workshop, an institution that seeks to encourage reading in Palestinian communities through creative writing projects and storytelling with children and teachers. She contributed to and wrote a foreword for *A Bird is Not a Stone: An Anthology of Contemporary Palestinian Poetry.*

Born in Hebron in 1965, **Khaled Hourani** is an artist, curator, critic and journalist based in Ramallah. He is the founder of Al Matal Gallery, founding director of the International Academy of Art in Palestine, and a former General Director of the Fine Arts Department in the Palestinian Ministry of Culture. He is also the founder of the Picasso in Palestine project, and co-director of a documentary of the same name. In 2013, he was awarded the Leonore Annenberg Prize Art and Social Change in New York. This is one of his first pieces of published fiction.

Ahmad Jaber holds a Master's degree in Civil Engineering and is a winner of the Abdul Qattan Foundation Award for Young Writer 2017 for his story collection *Mr. Azraq in the Cinema*. He has published stories in many local websites and newspapers.

Ziad Khadash is a Palestinian writer. He was born in 1964 in the village of Beit Nabala, and lives in the Jalazoun refugee camp near Ramallah. Khadash holds a BA in Arabic literature from the University of Jordan and works as a creative writing teacher in schools in Ramallah. He is author of 12 short story collections, the most recent of which was *Overwhelmed by Laughter* (House of Everything, Haifa). His story 'Wonderful Reasons to Cry' was shortlisted for the 2015 Kuwaiti Al-Multaqa Prize for the Short Story.

Ibrahim Nasrallah was born in 1954 to Palestinian parents who were evicted from their land in Palestine in 1948. He spent his childhood and youth in a refugee camp in Jordan, and began his career as a teacher in Saudi Arabia. After returning to Amman, he worked in the media and cultural sector until 2006. To date, he has published 15 poetry collections, 21 novels, and several other books. In 1985, he started writing the *Palestinian Comedy* covering 250 years of modern Palestinian history in a series of independent novels. His works have been translated into English, Italian, Danish, Turkish, and Persian. Three of his novels have been shortlisted or longlisted for the International Prize for Arabic Fiction (IPAF) – sometimes referred to as the 'Arabic Booker' – and in 2018 his novel *The Second Dog War* won it. In 2012 he won the inaugural Jerusalem Award for Culture and Creativity, and his novel *Prairies of Fever* was chosen by *The Guardian* one of the ten most important novels written about the Arab world.

Anas Abu Rahma is a poet and fiction writer. He has two published YA novels, as well as dozens of short stories for younger children. His novel *The Yellow Corn Inn* won the Children's Book Publishers Forum Award. Whilst his book *A Story about Q & L* won the Etisalat Award for Children's Books.

Mahmoud Shukair was born in Jerusalem in 1941 and is one of the best-known short story writers in the Arab world, and his stories have been translated into numerous languages. His 45 books include nine short story collections and 13 books for children. He has also written extensively for television, theatre, and print and online media. In 2011, he was awarded the Mahmoud Darwish Prize for Freedom of Expression. His 2016 novel *Praise for the Women of the Family* was nominated for the IPAF. He has previously been the editor-in-chief of the weekly Jerusalem newspaper *Al-Taliah*.

About the Translators

Emre Bennett is a keen linguist and a fanatic reader of Middle-Eastern literature. He is an Arabic language graduate from the University of Westminster where he also completed his Master's in Specialised Translation. He attended the City University's 'Translate the City' summer course in literary translation and freelances as a translator while studying Middle Eastern and Asian languages in his free time.

Raphael Cohen is a professional translator and lexicographer. His most recent publications are the novel *Guard of the Dead* by George Yaraq (April 2019) and *The Book of Cairo* (2019) and, forthcoming in 2021, the novel *Madness of Despair* by Ghalya Al Saeed plus a selection of Ahmed Morsi's poetry *Poems of Alexandria and New York*. He contributed to *Blade of Grass, An Anthology of New Palestinian Poetry* (ed. Naomi Foyle, 2017) and has translated a number of novels including Mona Prince's *So You May See* (AUC Press) and Ahlem Mosteghanemi's *Bridges of Constantine* (Bloomsbury). He is a contributing editor of *Banipal*.

Raphael Cormack is a translator, editor and author with a PhD in modern Arabic literature. He is the co-editor *The Book of Khartoum* (2016), with Max Shmookler, and editor of *The Book of Cairo* (2019), both published by Comma Press. As well as other translations, he is currently working on a non-fiction book about the female entertainers of early 20th century Cairo, called *Midnight in Cairo* (to be published in May 2021).

Basma Ghalayini is a literary translator born in Gaza. She has previously translated short stories for the Commonwealth Writers, Maalboret, Deep Vellum Press and Comma Press (*Banthology, The Book of Cairo*). She was the editor of *Palestine + 100* (Comma Press), and co-editor of the forthcoming special Palestinian edition of *Strange Horizons* (2021).

Mohammed Ghalaieny worked for two years as reporter for New York based Free Speech Radio News in Gaza and as a presenter on Palestine Satellite Channel, conducting and translating live interviews and reports, and whilst in Gaza has volunteered regularly as a translator for the Union of Health and Work Committees. He was a contributing translator to *The Book of Khartoum,* and *Palestine + 100* (Comma, 2016 and 2019) and currently works in the field of air quality in the UK.

Alexander Hong is an Arabic-to-English translator who completed a Master's degree in Middle Eastern Studies and Arabic at SOAS, University of London. His first translation of Diaa Jubaili's short story, 'The Darwinist' was published in *Strange Horizons* magazine. He also translates for Fairtrade UK.

Thoraya El-Rayyes is a writer, literary translator and political sociologist based between Amman and London. Her English language translations of contemporary Arabic literature have won multiple awards, and have appeared in publications including *The Kenyon Review, Black Warrior Review* and *World Literature Today*.

Andrew Leber is a PhD Candidate at Harvard University's Department of Government, where he researchers the politics of authoritarianism in the Middle East and North Africa. His translations have appeared in outlets such as *AGNI* online, the *New Statesman*, the *Brooklyn Rail, Jadaliyya* and *Guernica*.

Yasmine Seale is a translator from the Arabic and French. She has previously translated poetry by Liwaa Yazji, Nizar Qabbani, Dakhtanus bint Laqit, Saadia Mufarreh and Aisha al-Qurtubiyya. Her first translated book, *Aladdin*, from the French of Antoine Galland, is forthcoming from W. W. Norton. She is currently working on a new translation of *A Thousand and One Nights* (for W. W. Norton); and a translation of the dream biography of the poet Badr Shakir al-Sayyab; and the letters of Ibn Arabi's Tarjuman al-Ashwaq.

Adam Talib is an award-winning translator of Arabic literature. He has translated four novels, including Fadi Azzam's *Sarmada*, Khairy Shalaby's *The Hashish Waiter*, Mekkawi Said's *Cairo Swan Song*, and Raja Alem's *The Dove's Necklace*, which he and Katharine Halls translated together. Other translations for Comma include Ahmed al-Malik's 'The Tank' in *The Book of Khartoum* (2015), Abdallah Tayeh's 'Two Men' in *The Book of Gaza* (2014), and Khaled Kaki's 'Operation Daniel' in *Iraq + 100* (2016). He teaches Arabic and comparative literature at Durham University.

The Book of Shanghai
Edited by Dai Congrong & Jin Li

The Book of Sheffield
Edited by Catherine Taylor

The Book of Tbilisi
Edited by Becca Parkinson & Gvantsa Jobava

The Book of Tokyo
Edited by Jim Hinks, Masashi Matsuie
& Michael Emmerich

ALSO AVAILABLE IN THIS SERIES

The Book of Jakarta

Edited by Maesy Ang & Teddy W. Kusuma

Made up of over 17,000 islands, Indonesia is the fourth most populous country on the planet. It is home to hundreds of different ethnicities and languages, and a cultural identity that is therefore constantly in flux. Like the country as a whole, the capital Jakarta is a multiplicity of irreducible, unpredictable and contradictory perspectives.

From down-and-out philosophers to roadside entertainers, the characters in these stories see Jakarta from all angles. Traversing different neighbourhoods and social strata, their stories capture the energy, aspirations, and ever-changing landscape of what is also the world's fastest-sinking city.

Featuring: utiuts, Sabda Armandio, Hanna Fransisca, Cyntha Hariadi, Afrizal Malna, Dewi Kharisma Michellia, Ratri Ninditya, Yusi Avianto Pareanom, Ben Sohib & Ziggy Zezsyazeoviennazabrizkie

ISBN: 978-1-91269-732-8
£9.99

The Book of Shanghai

Edited by Dai Congrong & Jin Li

The characters in this literary exploration of one of the world's biggest cities are all on a mission. Whether it is responding to events around them, or following some impulse of their own, they are defined by their determination – a refusal to lose themselves in a city that might otherwise leave them anonymous, disconnected, alone.

From the neglected mother whose side-hustle in collecting sellable waste becomes an obsession, to the schoolboy determined to end a long-standing feud between his family and another, these characters show a defiance that reminds us why Shanghai – despite its hurtling economic growth –remains an epicentre for individual creativity.

Featuring: Wang Anyi, Xiao Bai, Shen Dacheng, Chen Danyan, Cai Jun, Chen Qiufan, Xia Shang, Teng Xiaolan, Fu Yuehui & Wang Zhanhei

ISBN: 978-1-91269-727-4
£9.99